BONDS &
BOUNDARIES

BONDS & BOUNDARIES

DALE CORVINO

QUEERMOJO
A Rebel Satori Imprint
New Orleans & New York

Published in the United States of America by
Queer Mojo
A Rebel Satori Imprint
www.rebelsatoripress.com

Paperback ISBN: 978-1-60864-294-6
Ebook ISBN: 978-1-60864-295-3

Library of Congress Control Number: 2023945004

CONTENTS

ACKNOWLEDGEMENTS

The following stories were previously published, in slightly different form: "More Sequins than Cloth" in *Jonathan Issue 9: a Journal of Queer Male Fiction*, "Drowned River" in *A + U Magazine*, "Jesus Year" in *Saints + Sinners 2017: New Fiction from the Festival*, "Worker Name," "Raunch Daddy," and "Traumatic Book Review: Alive, by Piers Paul Read" in the chapbook *Worker Names* (Gertrude Press).

To my mom Marie for her boundless faith; to my beacon
Dean Johnson, whose salon "Reading for Filth" was the laboratory
for many of these stories, and to Jean-Pierre Lopez,
my companion in this afterlife.

PART 1: BEACONS

GREAT WHITE

"Where'd you get this, cuz?" asked Dante, pulling a worn paperback from a stack of items left on the curb. Freddy was moving into Dante's Brooklyn apartment, hauling boxes out of a rented truck. Originally the servant's hall, the room he was moving into was narrow but had three windows that extended past the brownstone's facade. He could stand at the front of the room and look up and down the tree-lined street like a sentry. Freddy was putting his possessions away neatly in a built-in cupboard, now repurposed as a closet.

"My mom…never got around to reading it though…"

"I read this when I was a kid," said Dante, inspecting the pages. "Spotted it sticking out of *my* mom's handbag. I reached for it—she smacked my hand without even slowing the car."

"Your ma see out the side of her head," said Freddy. Dante nodded.

"One of her superpowers. Her smacks left a sting."

"No doubt…"

Freddy and Dante had been close growing up even though Freddy was years younger. Their extended family was close back then, too: Sunday dinners in their grandmother's big Venetian-themed living room, the expressive emotionality of every gathering. She tended a garden and their grandfather caught crabs in traps in the creek that ran behind the property. Her meals were borne of this dual bounty of land and sea, her cooking impeccable. Their grandfather taught them to comb the reeds for mussels. As they grew up the mussel beds dissipated and the Italian-born generation passed on or else moved away; Sunday dinners came to an end. The cousins looked more like brothers, carrying the same warmed skin tone from their Sicilian fathers, the same crescent eyes, the same black waves rippling across their foreheads, the same compactness.

After Freddy was hired by a new media company in the former Navy Yard, Dante invited him over for a little celebration. He'd been commuting from Long Island during his prolonged job hunt. "I don't like Freddy back living with that holier-than-thou. You know what she called me?" His mom loved her son fiercely and took no shit from her sister-in-law, but he couldn't fully recruit her to his rage: "Connie's family…" Though Dante saw his mom at holiday dinners, he hadn't visited with her one-on-one in years. The day Dante told his mom that he liked men, she'd pulled him in close and whispered: *That just means you'll never leave me.*

Dante fluttered the paperback's dry pages.

"She stapled up Chapter Eight because of the dirty parts. See the little holes?"

"Oh word?"

"I took them out at night so I could read it," Dante recalled.

"Of course you did. Never did see that movie, think I was too young," said Freddy.

"That movie fucked me up, let me tell you. The theater was packed. Some girls in front giggled at the skinny-dipping scene, but they were screaming later. After the shark took little Alex off his raft, I ran to the

2

bathroom and puked my licorice. Stayed out of the ocean the whole summer and the next."

Only on very clear days on his town's ocean-facing beach could Dante make out the Twin Tower's beveled corners catching the light. That vision of thin gleaming strips beyond the vast Atlantic flashed in his mind. From an early age he'd set them as a beacon. His elders, whose nostalgia for their youths in Brooklyn was salted with bitterness, would shrug at these apparitions. They'd fled city life to the town of Long Beach—which over the years had declined from its former grandeur as a seaside resort—and none of them had ever gone back, not even for a visit. His grandfather's hurt complaint when he announced that he was moving to Fort Greene was still lodged in his chest: *I broke my back to get us the hell out of Brooklyn, you ingrate…*

"You always loved the water, like Grandpa…" said Freddy.

"Yea..After *Jaws*, I stuck to the Rec Center pool, but damned if I wasn't always running into one rule or another there. One day it was my cutoffs. Another for taking too much time on the diving board. The lifeguard blew his whistle and pointed to the 'one bounce only' sign I'd never even noticed it before. Ordered out of the pool for roughhousing when it wasn't even me, it was the older boys, splashing and pinching each other's nipples."

"What's so dirty in *Jaws?*" Abel asked as he snatched the book out of Dante's hand. Abel—Dante's ex who lived around the corner—had come by to help the cousins with the move. He flipped through the chapter. "Oh, right here: 'Ellen started to giggle again, imagining the sight of Hooper lying by the side of the road, stiff as a flagpole, and her-

3

self lying next to him, her dress bunched up around her waist and her vagina yawning open glistening wet, for all the world to see...'"

His audience groaned.

"Oh no, not right," said Freddy, shaking his head.

"I went to so much trouble for *that?*" asked Dante.

"Aunt Angie got out her stapler, huh?" said Freddy, laughing.

"Well, at least you came away from the reading with a healthy respect for sharks—and vaginas," cracked Abel. The cousins laughed, and the three headed inside.

It was after the celebration Dante threw for Freddy's new job when he'd turned to him and asked, "Why don't you move in here, cuz?"

"Hell with the Long Island Railroad!" answered Freddy, with mock seriousness and a raised fist.

"Take the front room. I'll give you a good rent."

"For real?" asked Freddy. Dante could track the weight of his offer breaking through his cousin's tipsiness.

"Just not sure how your ma's gonna take it."

"Don't worry about her...I got this," said Freddy.

Dante smiled. "That's why you're my number one, cuz," he said, initiating their handshake. Freddy was the only family he spoke to any more other than his mom.

One sunny morning, shortly after Freddy had moved in, Dante entered the living room to find him getting ready for a bike ride. Freddy smiled at his cousin expectantly as he fussed with the seat. Dante sensed that Freddy was holding space for him to talk about Abel and instead got silence.

"Okay, gonna hit the park," Freddy said. Dante held the front door open for him wordlessly, and Freddy pushed off.

Upon first meeting Abel, Freddy had asked, "So how did you two meet up? At the store, in the park?"

"It *was* the park," Abel answered, giving Dante a sly look. "After dark. Know why I picked up your cousin?"

"Because I'm fine." Dante said, preening.

"Ok, that was a factor. Everyone else was on the hunt, but your cousin stood in one spot looking at the moon."

"He howl any?" Freddy joked.

Dante cut off Abel's shot at innuendo. "We quickly realized we make better friends than anything else."

"Well, that's one take," Abel said with an eye-roll.

"So it's like that…" said Freddy. "Cool, cool." His brow furrowed as he processed this new information about the sexual ecosystem of gay men.

Abel talked Dante into going dancing. "There's a party right down the street, in the old Tennis Club, classic house all night…" He enjoyed it for a time but left first, while his indefatigable ex carried on. Walking home, his firm body ached from hours of dancing and his limbs swayed loosely through the night air. He paused in front of the brownstone to gaze through the tall windows of the living room glowing like a lantern. He'd found this apartment the day he landed a job at Google as an Account Manager in the Fashion Vertical, when the company first opened a New York office. "A stylish cat who knows his analytics," the hiring manager had enthused at his interview, "a unicorn."

Though many original features of the apartment were intact, the had seen signs of hard use here and there. He and Freddy had spent a week fixing it up; then, on an all-nighter, Dante had dry brushed the walls with milk paint, letting old hues and wallpapers show through. He'd furnished it with mute black pieces, giving a stark effect. "This the waiting room in Ghostland," was Freddy's assessment upon seeing it finished and decorated.

He cautiously peeked in the window of Freddy's room; the sight of his cousin sleeping soundly brought him a rare contentment. He spotted the paperback on top of the discard pile at curbside, balanced on an outdated PlayStation and a pile of floppy disks. Avoiding the creaking floorboards, Dante padded to his bedroom, rescued paperback in hand. He undressed and rubbed his limbs up and down, first his calves, then his thighs, then each forearm and bicep with the opposite hand. They were pliant in an unaccustomed way, making them feel like someone else's. He usually held himself so tightly.

More than anything, Dante wanted his cousin to be happy in his home. All those years on his own pushing to get ahead he hadn't meant to leave everyone else behind. The night of the celebration, Freddy had arrived with a bottle of whiskey in one hand and a box of tarallucci in the other. The latter was an inside joke between the cousins, because one night on a sleepover they'd swiped a box of the hard biscuits hidden away in Aunt Connie's pantry. They'd planned on having just one each but wound up finishing them. She'd chased them around with a wooden spoon after finding the empty box, yelling, "Sneaks! Those were for company!" The box prompted immediate recall of that teenage misadventure; the cousins had talked over each other and their laughter telling the story to Abel, and then took to celebrating.

"This round's for making it to your first pay period," Dante had said as he handed them whiskey cocktails.

"Got my direct deposit, look out."

"Dante's got some mixology skills, huh Freddy?" asked Abel.

"A pop-up bar cabinet, that's some James Bond shit," he'd answered, admiring his cousin's style. "Your dad would have loved this set-up."

"Yea," answered Dante, awash in another childhood recollection. Dante's father—compact, muscular, swarthy, with a full head of hair he kept in a pompadour even as it turned silver—had gotten his start in business hand-cleaning this bar near his house, the Keyboard Lounge. One Sunday, Dante had accompanied his father to the bar. Upon meeting Dante, the owner's son threw some spare change under the barstools, prodding Dante to search for the money his customers had lost on the sticky floor. From the back room where he was cleaning, he father just shook his head.

Freddy had rapped the table to bring Dante back to the present. Abel appeared from the kitchen with an elegant platter, exclaiming, "The delights of your youth, dressed up with French cheese and grapes." Freddy attacked the platter, saying, "This cat's funny. And upfront. Not like my cousin…all circumspect." Dante flinched at Freddy's assessment, then popped a grape.

Dante slipped under the covers with the paperback, its binding cracked. As he scanned the foxed pages of this artifact from childhood, memories crept into his Ghostland chamber. Unlike the warm reminiscences the peppery tarallucci had elicited, these were knotted and dark. The glowing walls were traced with fugitive scenes from childhood, colors of a faded Kodachrome: seagulls hopping on the damp sand of the receding tide; his grandfather's plum tree dropping fruit on the patio; his mother in a patchwork denim pantsuit racing him to the car…

It was that second ocean-less summer when the Youth Rec Manager—a college student from Lido Beach who smiled a lot—took him up to the mezzanine, still dripping wet. He pinned him and tugged at his swim suit. Dante fixed on his chest, with its cross-shaped pattern of curly black hairs. He felt his hard-on between his thighs and his hot breath on his neck. His own hard-on slipped off his belly. The older teen's musky smell drove out the chlorine burn, his hairiness on him like a blanket against the cold block wall.

He saw the face of Mrs. Chiaramonte, the lady who'd lent his dad money, when he went with this father to deliver roses on her birthday. She'd taken the flowers and set them on a mirrored table, which reflected them in multitudes. "Aren't you *adorable*," she'd fussed over him more than the flowers, crouching to give him a hug. She smelled of face powder. Her black hair was curled in a bouffant, and a beauty mark hung over her painted lips like punctuation. Her skin was the color and shine of the linoleum floor at the supermarket, the lightest pink. She smiled at Dante with her giant teeth.

Next in the line of hard knots working its way through his clenched throat: the day his dad came home from her town, the town on the bay, the safe town, the rich town, shaking with rage. He'd watched him tell his mom from the next room.

"That smug banker. Thinks he's one of them…I was making a payment just like every month. He insinuated that we were carrying on—in front of his son no less. He backed down when he saw me steaming, and do you know what he said? 'Anyways she's too snooty to go for a cleaner…' That *sfaccimma*…"

It was a curse his mother used freely. Dante once asked her what it meant and his uncle volunteered a mangled translation: *cum face*.

He'd watched his mother stroke his father's head.

"*Sfaccimma!*"

His father straightened up when he spotted Dante through the doorway.

The night with the paperback flashed in his mind as he pressed his fingertips into the staple holes. He'd hoped to conquer his fear of the ocean by reading the story through—but then he got to the gleaming row of staples.

"Ma?"

"Yeah, that's the adult part. You're too young for that. Anyway, it's not even in the movie," she answered.

He'd removed each staple one by one, slowly and carefully bending their legs, pulling them out by their crowns, without tearing the pages. Their teeth stabbed at his tender finger pads. He saved them in an empty matchbox, planning to put them back in before returning the book. He stayed up all night reading, including Chapter Eight, in which Chief Brody's wife has an affair with stiff-as-a-flagpole Hooper. He rushed its pages before the sun came up, then pushed the staples back into the little holes one by one, bending them back into shape. His fingertips bled a little from the pricks of the staples' teeth, and he took care not to stain the pages.

This latest recollection of those pricks set off the nerves in Dante's now-hardened fingertips, which grasped too late at the book as it slipped away and fell to the floor. He rubbed his arms again. There was still soreness from dancing, but they had reset back to their usual tightness. He tugged at his erection, turned off the lamp, and shuddered at the giant menacing body in his bedroom. It was solitude in the borrowed form of a Great White, his room a tank unable to contain it. He turned over and ran through figures until sleep overwhelmed him.

As light snuck past the curtains, Dante awoke. It was Sunday. He dressed and crept quietly into the kitchen, not wanting to disturb his cousin, but Freddy was already up and in the kitchen. Freddy smiled, squinting through remnant sleepiness, and noticed his cousin was dressed in good clothes. He filled a thermos with coffee and handed it to Dante with a wink.

"Going back to Long Beach? Give Aunt Angie a hug for me…"

"You know it, cuz," answered Dante.

Dante stepped out into the sun-dappled street and came upon Abel on the corner. His skin was damp and glowy, his tight curls dewed with sweat. He'd been up all night and was chatting with Medhi from the bodega, a straight kid who enjoyed gay flirting. Dante gave Abel a hug.

"A PDA from you? What's the occasion?" Abel asked, but Dante just smiled.

Abel picked a bouquet of cosmos from the row of flowers on display and handed it to Dante. "On me," he said to Medhi.

Dante continued to the station. The day she'd called him around dawn surged his shores: *Your father, Dante…He held in so much he burst…*

He'd dropped everything and ran to the station. She'd been otherwise composed through her grief, but at times gripped his arm so tightly her nails left marks. He kept up on visits for some time after but it felt like an affront when she moved in to the senior apartment with Connie, who had all but called him an abomination. The visits had soon after stopped. A cut of every paycheck still went into her account, direct deposit.

Dante continued to the station and boarded the train to Long Beach. He poured all of his selves into the vinyl seat: the lost one, the damaged one, the one who'd pushed through, the little boy always trying to please her. The conductor punched his ticket.

As the train lurched from station to station, he opened the thermos carefully. Holding the cup of hot liquid set off phantom pricks on his finger pads—guilt over the deception of the staples—but with each mile traveled the feeling lessened. The train pulled in to the transfer station. He moved the bouquet from the seat in front of him to allow a woman and her child to sit, inhaling its grassy, chocolatey scent. Abel had given him the same flowers once before, and the symbolism of it had made him uncomfortable. "Are you ever going let me love you?" Abel had demanded, to silence. "At least smell them," he'd punctured it as he walked away.

He scanned the cluttered backyards of the houses abutting the tracks as the train pulled out of the station of the town where Mrs. Chiaramonte had lived and died, the town on the tranquil side of the bay. Her smug banker bastard of a husband had looked down upon the Sicilian floor cleaner and so had he, for too long. He'd gone for the sticky coins off the floor instead of the lessons his father was offering about dedication and purpose. His dad hadn't lived to see him find his footing. Dante kept an old photo on his desktop of him in his coverall embroidered with the company name, standing tall next to his floor polishing equipment.

He texted his mother: 'LB 5 min.' Angie Rizzo was born Angelica Carrera, having married his father over the objections of her mother; the couple eloped to California. Dante had grown up aware of the underlying tensions but never grasping the cause until his mother had lashed out at his dad's wake: "You never once gave him a chance…You called him 'the African' the day you met him and never stopped…" His grandmother's eyes had pleaded with him through his mother's tirade, but all those years of her sheltering him had turned to betrayal in that instant.

Angie was frying *arancini*—her mother-in-law's recipe—when he'd come home from the pool after the run-in with the Youth Rec Manager. She'd looked at him, or more like *through* him, her full eyebrows raised to the ceiling, until the smoke alarm went off. The next morning she took him to the ocean. Slipping off her sundress in the parking lot, she had on a one-piece swimsuit underneath: pink, belted, with a row of fringe along the legholes. She wordlessly shimmied into the water until he relented and jumped in.

The train slowed and the conductor announced, "Long Beach, last stop, everyone off," over and over as the train emptied. Angie was waiting for him at the head of the platform wearing one of her sharp pantsuits. Recovering from knee surgery, she held herself up on a walking stick, but seemed to spring off it upon spotting him walking towards her. Color and light returned to her face as if clouds had drifted away. Failing to hold back his tears, Dante lowered himself back into her arms, back with his shark and his police chief, his library and his censor. Though weary, she'd retained her superpowers, and he would never leave her.

MISS BENSONHURST

Mrs. Helen Guagliardo of Island Park sunk to the floor, sobbing in front of the television—a brand new color console model she would never watch again. She wore a leopard print dressing gown and kept her hair in a sweeping bouffant, which resolved into a single large curl on one side. Her mouth was painted red. Her creamy skin had lost its color and tears tracked through her eyeliner. Her mime-like reflection startled her when she caught it in the smoked mirrored console on the wall opposite. Clutching a pair of black leather stilettos to her breast, she murmured, "Poor doll...poor doll," through blackened tears. The phone rang eleven times but she wouldn't answer.

The atomized grief peculiar to the passing of a beloved figure hung all over the country, but Helen was seized by a loss both personal and manifold. She'd lost her friend twice before; once after she'd entered into an ill-advised marriage, and again when the fury of her fame would not relent. Now those knotted old losses felt permanent. As the television flashed newsreel footage of her friend entertaining troops in Korea, Helen ran her own newsreel projection of how she came to meet the beauty whose picture hung in her vestibule. *It was in San Francisco, while living that darling bungalow.* She'd pushed her husband to relocate out west, to get away from her domineering mother. That was until the big earthquake hit.

"You're not marrying that *Africano*," was what her mother had hissed, in reply to her proclamation that she had fallen in love with Antonio Guagliardo, a Sicilian. "He's a good catch, Mama. He's getting a law degree on the GI bill," she pleaded. Helen had never been so angry with her nor felt so defiant. She seethed. It was true that Antonio was swarthy, while Helen's milky complexion was a point of family pride. Helen had fallen for his good looks and his wavy pompadour, but she'd come to love him for his quiet dignity. He was smarter than any of the other boys in Bensonhurst. She'd held her tongue while glaring at her mother through narrowed eyes, her teeth clenched.

They'd eloped the following week and moved into their own apartment on Manhattan's West Side. Antonio had a position in the legal department of an international trading company. Helen worked as a buyer for a fashion house, something else her mother disapproved. They visited his family on Sundays, and while Helen's brothers would occasionally stop over, she did not see her parents for a full year after the marriage. Her brother Romeo didn't share his parents' bias.

"I like your lawyer well enough, but I really like his mama's *arancini*," he said, licking his fingers.

"Tell them I'm expecting," Helen had whispered to him as she kissed his cheek goodbye. "*Madonna mia*, you're gonna give her a heart attack," replied Romeo, as he shook Antonio's hand.

Romeo had brought his fiancée to meet his mother the following Sunday. "Hello, Signora Camera," she greeted her future mother-in-law with deference. Everyone called her that because she was from the old country and she was formidable. It had pained her to leave her home in Amalfi, to board a steamship with her young children for a journey across the sea. She was picking herbs when Romeo gave her the news. She clenched the rosemary sprigs tightly, releasing their aroma. Romeo tried following along with what his parents were saying, although his comprehension of the rapid-fire exchange was incomplete. The family had emigrated when he was just eleven and he'd grown up in the streets of Brooklyn, running with Irish and Polish kids. He certainly understood "*Que vergogna*," (what a disgrace), which she yelled repeatedly. The name of the priest at Holy Angels was summoned repeatedly. "It's a blessed event, Mama," cried Romeo, surprised that the news hadn't softened her stance.

Helen had named her son Sergio–after her mother's father–and an icy detente was forged. Even when her second, a daughter, was born, little of her mother's outlook had changed. She was nothing better than curt with Antonio, and she'd turn away and give her own daughter a cheek whenever she kissed her. That she was withholding with her grandchildren was something Helen could not forgive; so when Antonio's company offered him a position in San Francisco, she jumped at the chance to move away from her rigid disapproval.

The young family had settled into a bungalow in the Sunnyside section. Antonio's company imported products from all over Europe. There had been some unrest on the docks under the last manager.

"Overseas commerce–you've got this, we want it–will go a long way towards getting this world back to normal," Antonio told the dockworkers now under his helm.

"Did you serve, Mister Lawyer?" One of the stevedores–a real smart-ass–had challenged him.

"Reggio, 'forty-three. Can you believe they sent me back there? Tripped up a team of Jerry infiltrators in U.S. uniforms with baseball questions," he answered, chuckling. The men laughed along. "The wife did her part, too. Brooklyn Navy Yard switchboard operator," he added. Their laughter subsided. "The Army even issued me an Italian phrasebook," he added, "Illustrated! It was good for a laugh," as he pulled it out of his jacket and showed it around. From that day forward, the dockworkers respected him, and Antonio thrived in his new position.

The day her phone was installed, Helen had called her brother.

"We've got a darling bungalow out here. You should see the back-yard! This area's full of Italians, Romeo."

"Is that a good thing or a bad thing?"

"Oh stop! Our neighbor, Marie DiMaggio, is Sicilian. She's a dear. Her father owns a fishing boat, docks it right in the wharf…" said Helen.

"Yea? That sounds like the life."

"You might know of her brother Joe…" she teased.

"The Yankee Clipper? You're pulling my leg."

"Come out and see us! Tell mama I'm fine," she said as she hung up. They'd found familiars in their new surroundings and were unburdened by family discord.

Soon after, Romeo had brought his family out and found work on the wharf, thanks to Mr. DiMaggio's connections. He needed to get out of Brooklyn for reasons not entirely clear to Helen. "The less you know, the better," he'd said of the matter. They rented a house in the neighborhood, and their children played together at one house or the other. Helen missed working; she liked having her own money and clamored for the stimulation of the business world. She enjoyed dressing up for work, too.

Marie DiMaggio had taken to Helen's young daughter—also named Marie—with her bright eyes and black curls. She was especially drawn to her young namesake as a protector. Marie came over to Helen's for lunch one day, and little Marie clung to her. While unpacking, Helen had come across a photo taken when she was seventeen and had entered into a local beauty pageant. Her hair was wavy, her curves ample, and she had a birthmark just above her mouth. It was punctuation on her pleasing face, like the dimples bracketing her smile.

"Oh! That darling one-piece and wedge heels," Marie exclaimed.

"And my sash. I still have it somewhere. The photographer posed me three-quarter, to show my better side," said Helen.

Little Marie, standing on her toes, imitated the pose in the pictures, to their amusement.

"She has your good looks, but sun-kissed," Marie noted of her namesake, as she examined the photo. Helen at first beamed at the comparison, but winced when remembering her own mother.

When Joe had begun courting the film star Marilyn Monroe, it was big news in the DiMaggio family and even bigger news beyond. The day Joe brought her to Marie's house for a visit, Helen was over. Her children were in the back yard, playing with their cousins and some of Marie's nieces and nephews. The men were out picking up a jug of wine from a neighbor who made his own. Joe went outside to play with the kids, and Helen's boy, a diehard Yankees fan despite his recent relocation, was awestruck. Joe autographed his baseball and tousled his hair.

Marilyn had stayed in the kitchen with the ladies. Helen thought that the movie star would be snobbish around them, but instead found her eager to fit in.

"You know, Helen did some modeling, too," said Marie.

"Oh, stop…" replied Helen.

"Did you? That's how I got my start," said Marilyn.

"Just a bit, for a bridal shop in Bensonhurst, mostly," replied Helen. She unwrapped her tray of lasagna.

"She was a beauty pageant contestant, too," added Marie.

"I can see why, she's a beautiful woman," said Marilyn.

Helen had looked at the woman before her, for the first time seeing her and not the person she'd seen on magazine covers. They were about the same age and height. Underneath her confection of platinum hair, her eyes were soulful, while her mouth trembled a bit, her body restive. She caught her gaze and said, "Aren't you a doll to say that," and smiled warmly. Marilyn studiously parroted her new friend's Brooklyn accent, which made them all laugh, though Helen blushed a little, too.

"I hope you're staying for supper, Helen's lasagna is to die for," said Marie, and she went off to find Joe.

"It looks wonderful," said Marilyn.

It was just that summer when Antonio had taken Helen to see *Gentlemen Prefer Blondes.* "Not my type of picture, but it was enjoyable," he'd said of it afterwards. Helen had gone into the theater a fan of another dark-haired beauty, Jane Russell, but left impressed with Marilyn's vamping performance. Several of the issues in her magazine rack had cover photos of Marilyn, too. She didn't know it, but Sergio had pawed over the inaugural issue of *Playboy*—especially its racy centerfold—with some boys from the old neighborhood. When he was sent inside to wash up, he was astounded to find her in the kitchen talking to his mother. He blushed instantly and could barely make it through a stammering, "Pleased to meet you."

"Could you show me how it's made?" asked Marilyn of Helen.

"I'm happy to," she replied.

The cooking lesson would have to wait for another day. Joe came in and took Marilyn away. "We're stopping in on Vince next," said Joe, referring to his older brother. He searched Marie's eyes for approval; despite her worries, she couldn't help but beam when thinking about Marilyn. He nodded to his sister in acknowledgement as they left.

The next time Marilyn and Joe spent a weekend in San Francisco they'd planned Sunday dinner at Marie's. Marie made her mother's *arancini* recipe, and Helen did the rest of the cooking. Marilyn drove by in her new Pontiac convertible to pick up Helen and the big pot of sauce she'd made. Helen was running back and forth between stirring the pots and fixing her hair when Marilyn knocked at the back door. She embraced Helen like an old friend, and removed her headscarf and sweater.

"Goodness, that smells wonderful," she said, taking in the aroma coming off the stove.

"Taste it for me," said Helen, offering her a spoonful.

Marilyn raised her sunglasses, then blew on the spoon and tasted. "Mmmm, I just love the flavor. It has a sweetness," she said.

"Marie's tomatoes," Helen said. "You start with garlic in oil, not too brown. Then an onion, the tomatoes–take the skins off–a bay leaf, fresh basil. Salt, pepper." Then she added, confidentially: "If your tomatoes aren't sweet, add a little carrot," and Marilyn smiled. She grabbed a handful of parsley and threw it into the pot. "And the final touch–fresh chopped parsley–the flat leaves, never curly!" she insisted. "Oh! I'll remember!" replied Marilyn, giving a little salute, and they both laughed. Helen packed the sauce and the meats in containers and Marilyn put them in a crate. On the kitchen table was a box of photos and mementos.

"I pulled that out of the attic. I was looking for my sash, it's somewhere in there," Helen said of the box.

"Where was this?" asked Marilyn of a photo on the stack. Helen came over to examine it.

"This was in front of the office building where I worked, on Fifth Avenue in Manhattan."

"Oh?"

"Yes, I was a buyer for Hattie Carnegie Wholesale," Helen elaborated.

"You're so photogenic. I love your dress," said Marilyn.

"Aren't you a doll!" She handed Marilyn her sweater. "That is my good side. You couldn't wear halter dresses to the office, but a sweetheart neckline I could get away with."

"I do so admire you, Helen. You have your beautiful family, and you're your own woman," said Marilyn. "Here's your sash!" she said, as she pulled a roll of watermarked blue satin from the box. "Miss Bensonhurst 1943," she read off the inscription as she unfurled it, then draped it over Helen's shoulder.

"The one and only!" Helen said, striking the three-quarter pose with a laugh. She gathered up her handbag. "You admire little Miss Bensonhurst? But you can have everything you want, dear," she said.

Marilyn laughed ruefully. "When they find out what I want, they hold it out further away," she said with a gesture.

"Who?"

Marilyn took Helen by the shoulders, and answered with mock seriousness, "The jackals…"

"Oh, them—they can go frig themselves!" answered Helen.

"Oh my!" reacted Marilyn. Shock turned to laughter, and Marilyn gave Helen a mock scold. "I'm going to remember that the next time I get called to the boardroom," she said, putting on her sweater.

"I have a mouth on me, I forget sometimes…" said Helen with a grin, as she picked up the crate. Marilyn lowered her sunglasses and gave Helen a sultry pout.

"So do I," she whispered the phrase breathlessly, sending up her own sex appeal. She and Helen broke out in laughter on their way to the car.

Once on the road, Marilyn raised the subject again.

"Vince is coming, you're getting the full DiMaggio once-over today..."

"I can make a good wife for Joe," said Marilyn. "Mrs. Marilyn DiMaggio..."

"Excuse me for saying, but Joe's a *testardo*..."

Marilyn gave her a quizzical look.

"He's stubborn, a mule. He wants an old-fashioned Italian housewife, like his mother," Helen explained.

"Well...I'm taking some time off from pictures..."

Helen held her tongue. She smiled at her friend, and touched her shoulder.

Some weeks later, Helen had gone back to Marie's house. She was watching her niece Loretta while her mother was at a doctor's appointment. Romeo's wife had stopped in with her newborn. Little Marie and Loretta were about the same age and played endlessly when they were together, games of their own invention that picked up from just where they left off. Marilyn stopped in while Joe was busy with his brothers. Helen had watched as the troubled expression she'd entered the room with fled her face once she crouched down to greet the girls. "Why, I don't think I've ever seen two girls as darling as you," and they'd smiled and swayed their little bodies. She immediately joined their game. They had a View-Master and for every picture on the reel, they would invent scenarios.

"I wanna go on the Fairy Wheel," said Loretta, looking through the View-Master.

"I do too!" added Marie. Marilyn laughed when she looked through the View-Master.

"Ah, the Fairy Wheel! They have one at Playland. Would you like

21

me to take you there?" she asked them.

"Yes," they cried collectively.

"Isn't that nice of Miss Marilyn, girls?" asked Helen, and the girls nodded in unison.

Marie agreed. "It'll be good to get them out of the house," gesturing towards the sleeping newborn. The trio took off to the amusement park, just past Golden Gate Park along the coast. Marilyn put her headscarf and dark sunglasses back on as a precaution. As they were admitted at the gate, they saw the Big Dipper roller coaster and the Shoot-the-Chutes ride in the distance, but the girls only had eyes for the Ferris Wheel.

Marilyn had spotted a photo booth and said, "Come on darlings, let's take a picture." She dug a quarter out of her purse, and they all squeezed into the booth, laughing. It was nice to be close to them and not to worry about the crowd for a moment. As they waited for the photo to process, a sailor recognized Marilyn from that *Playboy* pictorial. He kept it respectable once he saw she was with children, but raised his eyebrows suggestively once and again. She gave him an autograph, urging him with her expressions not to spread the word, glancing at the children. The photo dropped down behind the chrome bars; in it, little Marie held a composed smile while looking right into the camera. Her dark curls filled much of the foreground, while Loretta was caught unawares by the flash, looking out of frame with a half-smile. Marilyn laughed behind Marie's curls. As they headed off towards the Ferris wheel, a brisk wind loosened the headscarf from around Marilyn's neck and carried the chiffon off in quick strokes over the heads of the crowd and away. The people around her had already picked up murmurs of her presence from that sailor, now confirmed by the sight of her signature platinum bob.

"Look Jimmy, it *is* her!" one man said to his friend, as he turned his camera towards her.

Autograph seekers and picture takers began crowding her, and she quickly grew worried for the girls' safety. "Please...the children," she pleaded to the engulfing crowd. The commotion attracted the attention of the Ferris Wheel operator, who called the police. Two uniformed officers rushed in and escorted them out of the park. The only ride the girls had that day was on the shoulders of San Francisco policemen.

Upon their return to Marie's house, Helen said, "Back already? It's like you hadn't been gone at all." Marilyn, who'd broken out in a nervous rash, ran into the bathroom. When the policemen appeared at the door to explain what had happened, Helen seized with panic, then rushed to hug the girls. After making sure they were unharmed, she sent them into the sunroom for a rest. She thanked the policemen as she saw him out, then knocked on the bathroom door to find Marilyn wiping her eyes. "Are you all right, doll?" Helen asked and she took her by the shoulders, and reviewed her body for harm, too. She noted the red splotches on her cheeks and her forehead.

"Helen, I'm so sorry, I got recognized, and..."

"What is it with those animals? Everyone's okay, that's all that matters," said Helen and she hugged Marilyn, who crumpled with relief. Marilyn pulled the photo out of her purse and showed it to her. "Look how my daughter is upstaging you. Your agent won't like this!" Helen shrieked, and the women laughed.

Some months after the Playland incident, she'd watched the television reports of Marilyn and Joe's wedding at City Hall. "*Managgia*," she found herself saying reflexively. She went over to Marie DiMaggio's that Sunday with a tray of lasagna and Marie said of the elopement, "Romantic, huh?" but her mouth quavered, and Helen could see the hurt in her eyes. "Then they went to Japan," she said with a helpless glance upward towards her savior. Helen sensed that Marie couldn't bring herself to say what she really wanted to. "Tony and I eloped too, you know. My mother..." said Helen, gesticulating her exasperation with a shake of her raised fingertips.

The marriage went bad quickly and it became a taboo topic in Marie DiMaggio's house.

The day Marilyn announced that she was seeking divorce an earthquake struck San Francisco. Little Marie was in class at a girl's school run by Dominican Sisters, housed in a former convent. For hours, Helen had been sick with worry, not knowing whether her daughter had been injured. She hadn't been seized with panic like that since Playland. When she could make her way to the school—a complex of brick structures built in the 1800's—its prominent bell tower was swaying ominously, threatening to collapse with every aftershock. She spotted Marie with her classmates assembled in the courtyard; the nun led the girls further away from the tower. "*Basta!* I've had it! We're going back to New York," she muttered on the way back to the car, to Marie's confusion. Once in the car, she said, "I'd rather deal with your *testarda* grandmother than friggin' earthquakes!"

Antonio had requested a transfer back to the New York office and bought a newly-built house on Long Island, with a spit of beach along the inland waters. Helen stood out to her neighbors because she commuted to the city three days a week to work at Hattie Carnegie, and for the way she furnished her home. Her living room had pink walls, and the gilt sofa was upholstered in fuchsia, as were two matching chairs with swirling backs. The coffee table had mirrored sections which reflected the room in multitudes. "It's flamboyant, like a movie set," her pinched next-door neighbor declared, to which Helen replied, "Why thanks, cookie," knowing it wasn't exactly a compliment. Antonio kept out of the living room; he staked out the backyard in good weather, tending his grapes, or trapping crabs in the creek. In the winter, he retreated to his locked study upstairs. Sergio, an engineering whiz, turned the attic into a sprawling laboratory, while Marie had the front room upstairs. She'd grow up talking to the neighborhood boys out her window. The smile of the platinum starlet in the 25¢ picture presided over the stairwell, mediating the separate domains of Helen, Antonio, and their children. Once they were settled into the house, Helen and Marie DiMaggio corresponded regularly, but Helen never saw Marilyn again.

Her daughter had only the faintest recollection. One day after school, Marie sat at the coffee table, flipping through a magazine, when she came upon a story about Marilyn. In the accompanying photo, she attended a luncheon seated next to Nikita Khrushchev; the magazine made a red-baiting scandal of it, as if her sitting next to Khrushchev represented a breach of the nation's defenses. Helen came home to find Marie looking at the magazine; she herself had attended a luncheon, and wore a dark suit with those black leather stilettos.

"You remember Marilyn, don't you dear?"

"She's the blonde lady?" replied Marie, pointing towards the vestibule.

"That's right. Do you remember when you went to Playland?"

"Umm...I remember the police man's uniform," Marie struggled to remember. She touched the photo in the magazine. "I liked her hair. It smelled nice, like flowers," she offered.

"I'm not surprised you don't remember much about Playland, doll—you were only six. We never went there again."

"She was a nice lady, Mama. Did she go all the way to Russia?"

asked Marie.

Helen smiled. "She's been all over the world, dolly," she answered with a measure of remorse. "These shoes I'm wearing? She gave them to me," she added, turning a foot. "They're Ferragamo. I only wear them on special occasions. They're from one of her movies."

"You look beautiful, Mama," said Marie, beaming, and she got up to give her a hug.

"Thanks dolly," said Helen, moved. "Now help me out of them, they're killing me," she added, as she leaned on her daughter to step out of the shoes.

◆

Marie, now sixteen, returned home from school, history textbook in hand. She found her mother on the floor in front of the television. Just a few seconds of newsreel footage was enough for her to understand what her anguish was about.

"Did something happen to Miss Marilyn?" she asked, running a finger along the television console.

Helen wiped her eyes. "Oh dolly, I don't know what they're saying, an overdose…" she said, as she struggled to stay composed.

"I'm sorry, Mama, I'm so sorry," Marie said, hugging her, "She was your friend…"

"We had that time, dolly, yes," she answered. A torrent of recollection hit. "I don't know what happened. Maybe she was just studying me for her next part."

"You don't really believe that, do you Mama?" asked Marie.

"Oh, I don't know. She told me once she just wanted to be a good Italian housewife for Joe…" she hesitated.

"I think she loved you. She gave you shoes," offered Marie.

"That she did," said Helen, still clinging to them, smiling through her pain. "But she had some bad men around her," said Helen. Remembering her friend's turn of phrase, she muttered, "Holding out carrots on sticks...those goddamned...jackals."

"Who were the bad men?" asked Marie.

Helen picked herself off the carpet and took her daughter by the shoulders. "Marie, I want you to know something. Yes, she wanted something she couldn't have. The grass is always greener, right? But she was the most...*determined* woman I've ever known. Did you know she was a business woman? And you know how that goes," she said, as despair threatened to overcome her.

"I don't understand..." answered Marie.

"She protected you," she said, sobbing as she squeezed Marie tightly. They walked in an embrace to the vestibule, and Marie went up to her room.

Helen walked over to the 25¢ picture. Marilyn had smiled a thousand and some times for photos—always the practiced smile she'd learned in modeling school—but in this photo, she threw her head back a little and was caught in a moment of spontaneous joy. Helen's guests had marveled over the photo for years, and Marie was the envy of her school friends. "You poor doll," she said as she crossed herself. Then she kissed her fingers and touched her hand to the photo. Though she'd been passing it for years, only now it conjured a vision of her friend's abridged visit to Playland: *She and the girls are enveloped in the warm bakelite booth. A curtain shields her from the crowds. The two little angels share the hard seat. The camera—that possessed apparatus which would stalk her to the end—here blinks obediently. Flash.* Then the menace outside the booth struck her and Helen shuddered.

She walked to the kitchen, letting her disheveled gown fall to the floor. The belt got stuck as it fell so she threw it around her shoulder. Now in a black bra and girdle, she put on the stilettos and stepped into the high heat of a summer afternoon. Her runny eye makeup liquified under the sun. She descended the porch stairs and walked out into the backyard, sinking into the grass here and there but otherwise maintaining her poise. Sergio, startled at her appearance, watched her from the attic window. Marie followed her into the kitchen and watched her from the window over the sink while pouring herself a glass of water. There on an August day in Nineteen Sixty-two, Miss Bensonhurst 1943, wearing a blank sash, pageant-walked to the bulkhead and spit black tears into the sea.

MORE SEQUINS THAN CLOTH

I'm pretty sure Nikki Saint-Roch is a stripper. I thought I saw her in a momentary refraction through the coffee bar storefront pulling up to the curb: lithe, dewy skin, beautiful, guarded. I conjured her scent, like fresh cut flowers, enduring, even as she traveled back and forth between New York and Montréal for the good gigs. She'd mentioned in her email reply that she was headed back to her apartment in Rosemount; no doubt she'd made a savvy investment. She'd saved her dollars and bought into a small, well-maintained building in an undervalued neighborhood. Maybe a suitcase from a recent trip lay still unpacked on a bench by the bed, but the place was otherwise neat and uncluttered, a serene, comforting nest.

It was the late summer in 2010 and I'd found myself with a free upcoming weekend. An urge to travel to Montréal overcame me. I was in an apocalyptic mood and whenever this mood hit me, I'd think: *Canada will be spared.* "Run north," my inner survivalist would whisper. My passport was about to expire, too. I was really too broke to indulge in what was still leisure travel even if motivated by dark visions. I'd been laid off from my high-paying management position during W's recession and was barely scraping doing temp work, so I set myself to the challenge of going to Montréal as cheaply as possible. Craigslist was going to make this happen. I'd answered an ad offering a rideshare from

New York to my destination on the very morning I wanted to travel. "Chip in for gas, or help out with the driving and the gas is on me," read the ad.

Nikki Saint-Roch was the name of the person who'd posted the rideshare ad, as I learned when she responded to my meticulous, persuasive inquiry. I made a point of mentioning that I don't drink or use drugs, and offered to drive or chip in for gas, whichever best suited her needs. We arranged a meeting point. I wanted to tell the Nikki Saint-Roch in my mind about my past experience in the sex trade without over-sharing, and about my stripper friends, maybe she knew some of them? I imagined us bonding fast and hard over our shared experience during the six-hour drive. We'd tell each other our war stories and she'd totally hook me up in Montréal with a loving, supportive community of sex workers.

I met her on the appointed corner at the appointed time. The real Nikki Saint-Roch was highly caffeinated woman of about thirty in pleated jean shorts and a CompUSA t-shirt. She wore one of those leather holsters for her Blackberry on her belt, the kind with the swivel clip. Basically this Nikki was the opposite of the Nikki I'd imagined. She was American, not Québécoise. She was squat and chunky, not lithe, some kind of tech nerd, not a stripper; so much for my premonitions.

There was another passenger traveling with us: Romilla, a soft-spoken college student who lived in Bushwick. Romilla had already taken the back seat and pitched in for gas since she didn't drive.

"Should I take the front?" I asked through the driver's side window.

"Sure thing, welcome aboard," Nikki replied.

I climbed into the front passenger seat of Nikki's late model economy hatchback and we were on our way. Nikki managed the crowded city streets and got us onto the highway with a few deft turns. She logged about a hundred thousand miles a year traveling for her job, she told us. I was relaxed enough to turn around and have a getting-to-know-you chat with Romilla. She was an art major, a transplant from Pennsylvania. We were both easing into our rideshare experience, for it looked like we'd succeeded in negotiating the dodgy terrain of craigslist postings and found a winner.

With little prompting, Nikki told us that she was an IT specialist for the State Department. She was of Cajun extraction, born in New Orleans. That explained the French last name. While she didn't explain to us why she owned an apartment in Montréal, I assumed it was so that she could make a swift exit from the US at any given moment, due to the true nature of her work. I guess I was not done projecting fantasies on Nikki Saint-Roch.

The first sign of trouble appeared just past Ramapo.

Once we got on Interstate Eighty-seven, Nikki floored it; I mean she really floored it. I hadn't imagined her sensible vehicle could accelerate to eighty-five so quickly. I went into full vigilance mode, eyes like saucers, assessing the danger points in the sparse traffic ahead of us, my fingernails dug into the armrest. My right foot involuntarily tapped an imaginary brake pedal in the passenger's well as we approached vehicles. Vigilance ceded to panic when Nikki became distracted with her Blackberry—scrolling through emails, resetting the GPS, checking the weekend weather. She swerved wildly as the car came upon slower vehicles.

Romilla and I exchanged worried glances through the rear view mirror. After a brief meditation to quell the passenger-seat panic surging inside of me, I spoke up:

"Er, Nikki—would you like me to drive?"

"Oh, that'd be great! How 'bout you take us as far as the border, and I'll take it from there?"

"Sure thing!"

Nikki abruptly pulled onto the shoulder and we switched places. Ever since sideswiping a kindly grandmother while taking a curve too fast as a new driver, I've been extremely cautious and defensive. I cruised slightly above the limit, a speed unlikely to call the attention of troopers. I always signaled when changing lanes, and always kept a safe distance from other vehicles. My eyes were fixed on the road at all times, while both hands firmly gripped the steering wheel. Needless to say, I would not be distracted by handheld devices.

After scrolling through emails and deftly thumbing in some replies, Nikki passed out cold in the passenger seat. Through the rear view mirror, a relieved Romilla mouthed a nearly silent "thank you," and slumped into the back seat.

Just as we approached the border, Nikki awakened, refreshed from her long nap. We sailed through security on her enhanced clearance and continued north towards Montréal with Nikki back behind the wheel. Her driving was perfectly reasonable and attentive in Canada; maybe she could get out of speeding tickets in the States with her credentials, or maybe she was just rested. We slid into town, and Nikki dropped us off in front of Mille de la Gauchetière.

"Thanks for doing all the driving! I'm heading back to New York on Monday. If you want to go back with me, hit me up," and handed us business cards—sure enough from the State Department. I was now convinced this was a cover. I'd earned my keep doing the driving and made it to Montréal for nothing, but didn't think I'd be repeating the experience.

Romilla and I shared a moment in front of the tallest building in the city.

"Omigod, I'm so glad you took over driving. I feared for my life."

"Yea, haha. I'm sure she's a good driver, but too distracted for me. I don't want to completely throw her under the bus..."

"Yea—especially since I'll be taking it home," Romilla deadpanned, and we laughed that dark survivor's laughter.

At a Bixi rack, I purchased a seventy-two hour subscription. Montréal's bike-sharing network would be my sole transportation solution. I cycled Mile-End to the apartment I've arranged to rent for the weekend, another craigslist find. In addition to using their "rideshare" and "housing sublets/temporary" sections, their "personals men seeking men" section would be my means to meet men without going out to clubs or bathhouses. Nothing like anonymous sexual encounters on the edge of an apocalypse. Whether it was to earn a living or to seek salvation I'd always had the same mission. Maybe I was a compulsive or, worse, a sexual tourist, but I preferred to think of myself as a vector of pleasure and intimacy. I stopped at an Italian café on Rue Saint-Zotique and composed a personal ad while drinking a macchiato and watching an Italian soccer match on the flat screen.

I Bixi'ed over to the Musée d'Art Contemporain. Parlovr, a dirty pop trio, was playing, and slipped into the crowded concert event through the exit without being seen. It was fun wading through all the cute, scruffy, hipster boys and their girlfriends, goddesses of understatement all. A Norwegian guy was the first to respond to my ad. I checked out his photos as a gentle mosh pit, more like a cuddle party, formed around me. He was a bit older, with a lean, vascular body and a heavy piece. "Please come over right away!" his email concluded. I found his enthusiasm charming so I extracted myself from the crowd and biked up Rue Saint-Urbain; the air was redolent with a warm, yeasty aroma that reminded me of bagels. I must have been missing New York.

I forgot his name moments after he introduced himself; it just wouldn't stick to my receptors. The Norwegian was very turned on by my ripeness from traveling and biking around, and immediately licked me from head to toe in the vestibule. While I was being tongued everywhere, I had a look around, feeling that there were eyes on me from every direction. Squinting through the dim light, I made out a stylized bear carving, there a frog, there a badger, up there an eagle whose wings spanned almost the whole space. The Norwegian had a collection of totem poles leaning against the walls of his vestibule, taking up much of its space, even blocking at least one doorway. I wondered if they were authentic or carvings for tourists.

After some rigorous acrobatics on the Norwegian's sturdy bed we showered together. We dried off on his balcony, where he was growing some monstrous *Trompettes des Anges*, or *Brugmansia*, these giant, white, pendant, bell-shaped flowers that were in bloom all over Montréal. Their fragrance was intoxicating. The Norwegian told me you can hallucinate from smoking them, but we just smoked his cigarettes. "What's this neighborhood? I smelled bread, or something baking," I hedged. "Oh! There's a bagel place down the street. They use woodburning ovens. This is Le Plateau. It was the battlefield outside the city's fortifications in the early days." In the afterglow, the Norwegian got romantic and a bit clingy so I left.

Back in Mile-End, I met up with the guy who'd rented me a basement apartment for the duration of my visit, an old-world Italian. We shared our heritage stories and immigration myths, while peppering the conversation in our respective broken Italian, his French-inflected, mine Brooklyn Guido. I settled into the quiet and cave-like apartment; it was set back from the street and ideally situated. I slept deeply. In the morning, I bought vegetables and a box of currants at the Marché Jean Talon, so impressed with the region's farmers, I wept a little over their labor.

The next men-seeking-men encounter was Marcel, a native of French-Italian background. I met him at his house in le Village, the gay enclave. I proposed we go to the Centre Canadien d'Architecture because I wanted to see an exhibit I'd read about. It turned out he had free passes from his job at Loto Québec. We toured the CCA and agreed that we especially liked the trippy drawings of Iannis Xenakis, whose work bridged architecture, music, and physics. We then biked back to his place; Marcel on his fancy ten-speed, me on a Bixi.

Marcel was a bit of a pedant, in the French manner, but well informed. We went to his bed to enjoy sixty-nine, forming a swirl of hunger on his quilt. Marcel had the lean, fit build of a yogi and a good heart. It was beautiful to watch his pedantry dissolve in howls, to have his most animal aspect in my mouth. He invited me to a naked yoga class the next day at Mudra Force. I was intrigued.

I had in mind to go back to Le Village for the naked yoga class, but instead I set a date to meet up with Érick, who was originally from Chicoutimi, this small village to the North at the confluence of two rivers. He lived in Hochelaga, a student area. Érick was very lean and ripped with long hair, a full beard, and a very Gallic nose. He was an actor and a singer of classical music, and worked part time for the government-run liquor authority. He had several tattoos, and a slight muskiness from lounging around the house in sweats and smoking cigarettes. I told him about the Parlovr concert, which got us on the subject of the Canadian music scene, and he played this track by Arcade Fire called "We Used to Wait."

So I never wrote a letter/I never took my true heart/I never wrote it down

So when the lights cut out/I was lost standing in the wilderness down-town

Érick was interested in American politics; he asked me about Glenn Beck. When I told him I believed that Beck is an untreated alcoholic with anger issues and delusions he seemed relieved. I realized his question was a test and I'd just passed. To seal the deal I expressed support for Quebec's Separatist movement. This totally worked and we started making out and it was super sexy, like two sympathetic dissidents from neighboring countries. He bent over to lick my tit, and I did the same to him. "Oh! I like that. Nipple sixty-nine," he said in his charming Québécois accent. He took me to his bed to teach each other more of our secrets. Érick burned long and slow for sure. It only ended when I couldn't take any more, then he brought me a delicious tropical juice and a cigarette.

Érick told me about an exhibit at the Centre des Sciences in the Vieux Port, the ancient heart of the city, called *Sexe: l'expo qui dit tout!* "It's sex education for teenagers, but very well done, with beautiful eem-AHJ." I didn't get to go see it because by then I was fucking Juano.

Juano was a little heavyset and bore strong resemblance to Venezuelan dictator Hugo Chavez. I wasn't too attracted to Juano due to this, but one thing that intrigued me is that he did not present as gay at all. He looked like the most ordinary straight guy you'd find loitering around the stands at a baseball game. I won't go into too much detail about Juano because I don't want to be unkind. Suffice to say that Juano was inexperienced with men and our session was more instructional than pleasurable.

On my last night in Montréal, and though Juano was something

36

of a disappointment, I looked back warmly on the Norwegian, Marcel, and Érick. I took the Greyhound bus home since I did not want to ride back with Nikki the high-speed State Department employee. I booked online and had to print the ticket, but all the copy places were closed due to Canadian Labor Day. Someone suggested I go into a Couche-Tard because they had printers. A handsome and friendly boy with a scruffy beard printed my ticket for free, as long as I bought a coffee. He was doing the same for a beautiful woman dressed down in baggy sweat pants, with her hair under a bandanna. It turned out we both had tickets for the New York bus.

The beautiful woman boarded and took the seat next to me. Maybe she chose it because it was the first empty one she came upon, maybe because I was less threatening than all the other solitary men further back. We smiled politely at each other when as she settled into her seat, and as much as I wanted to talk to her, I gave her privacy.

After getting through customs, my seatmate stealthily pulled a pair of panties out of her bag and finished sewing sequins all along the waistline and the legholes. They were more sequins than cloth. I'd been party to this scenario before and couldn't help but smile but still don't want to intrude. She caught me smiling, and offered that she was a "performer" on her way to a booking. I said I was in Montréal because I had a premonition and was waiting out the apocalypse and she laughed. I told her about everything that came to me via craigslist ads: the ride with IT girl Nikki, the quiet apartment, the mostly hot men. *I think she gets me now, based on her wide smile.*

As I was rattling off the story of my adventure, she was pulling thread through the holes in little gold sequins. I watched as she labored introspectively and suddenly felt self-conscious about my story. What seemed like savvy resourcefulness now felt like egotistical indulgence.

37

I wanted to turn the conversation in her direction, but rather than ask the obvious "what kind of performer are you" question, I dropped the names of a couple of New York burlesque dancers I knew: Dirty Martini, the Pontani Sisters.

"Oh, I know those girls," she smiled. "I work under the name Kitten Infinite. Call me Kitty. This is me." She pulled a post card out of her bag, with a photo of her in stockings, sparkly panties, and big kitten paws cupping her breasts, posing in front of one those infinity mirrors. It was spectacular, and I got lost in her infinite smile as I held the card in front of me. After a minute, she took it back from me. "I only have the one on me," she explained. "I have to be careful at the border."

"Me too," I joked, but Kitty went silent. Her brow creased and her she stared out the window, a thousand miles past the solemn skyline of Albany, its blank towers like tombstones of unknown dead.

"Sorry. I had a bad night last night. This guy…"

Kitty put away her sewing and took some deep breaths.

"A drunk fucker at the club last night. He wanted a private show, which was stupid—it's not that kind of club. I've worked both, though. I told him no and turned away, and he slipped his dirty hand between my legs from behind, and…"

Kitty showed me what the drunk fucker did with his dirty hand, pulling her hand up sharply through the air like a knife blade.

"Oh. I'm so sorry…" Kitty's story took my breath from me and I choked on my inadequate response. She picked her head up.

"So is he. The girls took him outside and kicked the shit out of him. And they still had on their cowboy boots from the finale, a Western themed group number. So yea…the whole thing was fucked up."

I reached out for her, and we held each other's hands for the rest of the ride, like siblings traveling unaccompanied.

DROWNED RIVER

"Good morning, *papi*, happy Friday," Chiqui greeted the bakery owner, a giant Syrian man, who replied with a smiling "*Sabah an-nur*" and gave her a bag of mini-muffins from yesterday. She swung past the main Post Office and saw Mr. Terry, who was always kind to her, if a bit stiff. Mr. Terry lived in Elliot houses same as Chiqui. He worked the Post Office retail window for years and looked forward to taking his pension, "If they don't steal it from me first," he would say whenever the topic came up lately. Chiqui bounced along in her new butter yellow chevron top. The history lesson Tenté had given her about the words carved into the front of the Post Office came back to her: *Neither snow nor rain nor heat nor gloom of night stays these couriers from the swift completion of their appointed rounds.* "The words of an ancient Greek, telling his people about the Persian mail system, but of course the Gringos think it's about the Pony Express or some shit..."

Mr. Terry would take his smoke breaks by the loading docks. Chiqui was friends with his daughter, who'd been begging him to quit. That's why he would blush a little when she caught him. Some nights she'd see him outside of Elliot Houses, cupping a cigarette in his hand, and they would just smile at each other.

"Hi Chiqui, look at you all sunshine today," said Dolores, another retail window attendant.

"*Mira*, you changed your hair, I love it! Super fancy."

A worker Chiqui had never seen before was there. Chiqui introduced herself and asked him where in the building he worked. He answered, "I'm a handler..." and then shifted his tone to a husky whisper and asked her, "Do you like being handled?" while moving his hands around an imaginary mound in front of him and swaying. The sexual innuendo was more for the benefit of his friends, who guffawed.

He can't help himself, Chiqui thought. *I have the curves and the ass he wants in a little package.* Then she caught him clocking her jawline. She hadn't been able to do her contouring that morning because the bathroom was busy. She was going to do it at GMHC. She had on yellow leggings that match her new top. They fit her perfectly now. She turned from the handler and adjusted the line of sequins running up the back of her calves. *He wants my cutlets, but has to make it a joke in front of his friends.* They all laughed except Mr. Terry.

"*Mira tu paquetico,* mister postman," she said, shaking her ass at him.

The assembled group laughed more at her joke than his. *I've conquered another man,* Chiqui thought, smiling. She ran her hand up through her curls and bounced them, a victory shake. Dolores complimented her hair.

"*Gracias,* the curls are my own, they all have kinky hair on my mom's side, but they straighten. I put in this new color, Nice N Easy Natural Medium Golden Neutral Blonde, that shit is Nice N Nasty going on..."

"And your headband..."

Chiqui straightened it. "You know, *mami,* I made it from the hem of this blouse. I'm crafty like that. I love coordinated. The leather clutch in light gray elevates the look. I used Lemon Drop on my lids, it makes my eyes sparkle, *linda.*" She fluttered her lashes.

The handler, in some gesture of atonement, offered Chiqui a cigarette. She shared the mini-muffins: "I earned these with my sunshine and the sun shines on all."

Delores asked her about Mr. Terry.

"We go back a long way....I grew up with his daughter. He knows me since I was born..." she replied. What she didn't say is that he knew her as Jaime Manriques, that he still can't say her name without fumbling. He'd stop himself from calling her Jaimito, then his mouth would run out of batteries.

Mr. Terry's daughter was about the same age as Jaime, and they used to play together, until she got her titties, then she worried about what others would think about her hanging out with such a feminine boy. Jaime's small circle knew he was a girl. All the other Puerto Rican kids at Elliot called him *La Chiquita*, but they'd protected him too. Whenever Jaime left Elliot he'd get harassed. Mr. Terry's stepson gave Jaime a blade with a pearl handle. She still had it. He'd shown Jaime how to sharpen and polish it. She took the name Chiqui when she transitioned: "I took their shade and made it chic."

Music was coming from a food truck that fed the workers, so Chiqui launched into a little number. She used to do shows at Escuelita, a nightclub near Times Square where Latino families would sit at big round tables and watch drag shows, the adults drinking rum. She struck a pose, pointing to the bow on her head, then launched into the lip-sync. The smokers lifted their heads and brightened one at a time like sunflowers as I she performed a salsa slide through them. "*Devora-me otra vez, devora-me otra vez...*She says 'eat me up again,'" she said, translating for the Handler, giving him her best seductive look, but he'd gone mute since their standoff. Chiqui was bringing the number home when the crowd heard a shriek overhead. "Is that a seagull? Why is he shading me?" Everyone laughed, even Mr. Terry.

"*Mira cabron, no me atormentes,*" Chiqui yelled to the bird. Don't mess with me, asshole. The gull glided down in a spiral, landing on a 'No Parking' sign so close by. Chiqui locked eyes with the gull, taking in his majesty, the full white breast, the gray wings, and the yellow beak. How she loved a coordinated look. "This bird is giving me life. Where did you come from, are you lost?" She asked, throwing a mini-muffin.

The handler opened his mouth: "We're just a few hundred feet away from the Hudson, and along here, it's a mix of seawater and fresh. The Lower Hudson is actually considered a drowned river—a river overrun with salt water. That's why we get seabirds, like that ring-billed gull."

"Okay, professor," Chiqui smiled in reply to his lesson.

"The maintenance guys know all about them, they've been nesting on the roof," added Mr. Terry. "They're a nuisance."

Chiqui said her goodbyes to the Post Office smokers crew. She gave them her signature exit, throwing a hand up with a flourish and waving her little fingers in front of her mug. She walked over the West Side Yard, where the Long Island Rail Road stored its trains after bringing all the suburban papis to their office jobs. It was a noisy job site, a crew was laying a big deck across the whole yard, and building some more office towers for them. She was feeling herself but reined it in to get past them. Not soon enough though, because one stocky guy in a hard hat and a safety vest clocked her. Chiqui caught him eye-rolling and frowning at her, all the disapproval in the way his taut body shifted. She hurried past him, almost slipping out of her gorgeous Italian cork-heeled wedge sandals.

Past the Yard was a brutalist office building with sloping sides from the Seventies that used to have an ice skating rink on the roof. Chiqui used to skate there, and always thought the concrete building looked like the headquarters of a dark empire. GMHC, where Chiqui went for counseling and lunch, had moved into the building a while back. She stopped to greet some other clients standing in front of the building entrance gossiping, Tenté among them. They hugged fiercely, tall Tenté spinning her small body around. They held a loud kiki for everyone coming in and out of the building to overhear.

Tenté, from the Canary Islands was Chiqui's best friend. A handsome queen—lean, tall, elegant, with a nose that commanded his face like a monument in a square and sad, expressive eyes—he was trained as a dancer and worked at the café on Christopher Street during the week. On Sunday nights he'd get up in drag and host a talent show. Chiqui called his more experimental form of drag "art school confidential." She'd been more of an old-school pageant queen. "Loca, this construction worker cabron spooked me, but now I'm with my people and unbothered," Chiqui said to Tenté, emphasizing her words with a hair flip.

Next she told him about the big gull that almost ruined her number. "Oh, yes, I've seen them around here," he said. "It reminds me of Tenerife. Once I watched one at Los Cristianos beach swoop down and carry off a tostada from this kid's hand, and another pluck a catch right off a fishing line."

"*Gaviota! Gaviota! Maldita seas,*" Chiqui sang for Tenté.

"You're more pigeon than seagull, loca…"

"It's true, I'm a city bird, except I'm not common, even if I came up in the projects."

Tenté lived close to the big Post Office. He was in the station all the time, sending packages to his mom—fabrics, underwear. He had a tough time making friends there at first, but once he got past the workers' gruff fronts, he found their humanity. He'd been renting a small room on the cheap from an older queen who supported his artistry. Tenté often stared out his window at the office building on the corner, a regular plaid of bricks and glass, lights on this floor, lights off the next. He kept his room dark except for a candle. He could even see the river between the buildings and beyond, just a little segment.

After hot lunch, they went back to Tenté's. His roommate was out and Chiqui was happy to have the bathroom to herself: "I can beat my mug in peace here with your good brushes and this bomb magnifying mirror." Tenté could be depressive. Once again he started moping and staring out the window like an aged-out novela star. "What that postman said is the Hudson is a body half riverine and half marine. Trans, like us. *Transformista*, between two islands," he said, pointing to his reflection in the window. "Trans woman, also between two islands," he continued, now pointing at her.

"Yes, loca, tell it." She knew he was an artist in his heart.

"I am a vagrant gull," he over-pronounced the words, as if for his ESL teacher.

She returned to the dark empire headquarters with a fresh beat, leaving Tenté to his melancholy. GMHC served hot dinners on Fridays; tonight it was turkey. "Turkey for a pigeon, hey," she said to the server. After dinner, she walked home down Tenth Avenue. It was that summer night when the sunset aligned with Manhattan's grid. The setting sun was a disk burning at the end of every intersection over the pink New Jersey sky. Chiqui was skirting the trucks pulling out of the loading docks at when she clocked him.

(Back in his dark little room, Tenté was pondering the uncanny dislocation of hearing the gulls around the Post Office while carrying a package for his mother. It took him back to those languid days at Los Cristianos, and even further back, to time spent playing around the

Port in Tenerife, picking over littered remains of crabs left by flyovers, getting into a staring match with one menacing gull roosting on a rock, and the rough dock worker who'd lavished attention upon him. He was back on that secret boat trip with that rough man. The gulls trailed the boat in a broken echelon, taking advantage of the craft's upwash while keeping black eyes peeled for food.)

Chiqui was sure he was following her. *Not this shit again.* She had phantom pangs from the last beating, those two mean junkies who broke her lip and pushed her into the street until she crawled under a truck. They tried to kick her with their work boots. She could hear him panting and even a snide little laugh. She fished the blade out of her clutch, and once she had a firm grip on it, finger on the release, she ran like a bitch on fire. He chased after her, but she got ahead enough to turn back and look at him. *Who this ugly* cabron *in a leather jacket too big for him? Do I know him?*

(Tenté wondered about the future of the gulls around him. There was still plenty of open sky around, but not for much longer. The Post Office would soon be converted into a train station—another *transform-ista.*)

Chiqui stumbled in her wedge heels. The *cabron* took advantage and caught up. He grabbed her clutch; she popped her blade. As she reached for her clutch, he caught her by the hair. *"Aie! Déjame!"* He laughed and jerked her around, hard. He pulled her down so forcefully she almost went down on her back. He took advantage of the moment to feel her breasts, squeezing them hard, trying to break them. Chiqui broke out of her wedge heels so could regain her balance back.

(They were raising up commercial buildings, floor by floor, over the West Side Yard. That contractor who'd shaded Chiqui was work-ing on a pair of towers that taper away from each other, like two awkward strangers forced into close contact on a subway car. That's what it looked like in the illustration they'd plastered all over the site enclosure. "The sky turns solid all around me," Tenté lamented.)

Chiqui's roots were burning from all the abuse. She took a desperate step: cutting through her hair with her blade, as close to his hand as she can get. She didn't want to lose too much length. She thought she could do it with one clean slice, but it took two. He screamed on the second cut and tried to hit her, but was dazed to find she's broken free of him. She ran towards home.

(Tenté marveled at how their pitchy calls blocked out every siren, every car horn, every downshifting truck. He found himself surrounded by the vast Atlantic of his childhood on West Thirty-Fourth. The sea of his youth was a flat, soft vastness of blue reflections. The city outside was hard, patterned, vertical ruptures made of minerals and ores re-formed, like stalagmites dripping from hubris. The gulls had this auditory power to take him back, faster than a jet, more reliably than a carefully labeled package from his mother.)

Chiqui, running, saw Mr. Terry on the corner, smoking. He threw down his cigarette and ran towards her. He yelled out "HEY!" and the *cabron* froze. Chiqui turned to face him. He just stood there with her hair in his hand, broken wedge heels at his feet, looking stupid. She must have cut into his meaty palm because blood was running into her hair. She noticed some splatter on her leather clutch. "Oh if he ruined my good clutch, I will cut that *cabron* for real..." She started for him again, but Mr. Terry held her back.

(Tenté was always oriented toward the sea. It guided his life choices, his migrations. Staring morosely at his sliver of the river, he internalized the tidal pull. He floated above himself walking along the river while smoking a spliff. In his sativa reverie, he passed the hulking coffin

46

of the Convention Center, then took in the assault of pulsing noise and aviation fumes of the heliport.)

The cabron yelled insults. Mr. Terry took Chiqui by the shoulders and looked into her eyes, really looked. It knocked her back into the moment. "Are you hurt?" he asked, and she shook her head.

(Tente's phone rang, taking him out of his trance. Hardly anyone called him. He answered hello but it was immediately clear he'd been pocket-dialed. He listened for voices over the rustling of fabric against the speakers, then a dramatic scene, screaming, jostling. He yelled into the phone but no one could hear him.)

Her chest burned, and she couldn't stop panting. She cried when Mr. Terry embraced her, and the panic subsided. *I'm just going to lean on this good man and cry. This is what it's like.* Mr. Terry rubbed her shoulders like no man ever had. "He's getting away, should we…?" and she answered, "Just let him go." Mr. Terry her tightly and exhaled. "Oh, Chiqui." It was the first time he'd ever used her name. All the fear rushed out of her shaking body, all the love she'd served flushed her skin, blushing it pink like the New Jersey sky. *I am protected, respected, alive.* Then she heard a high-pitched squeak in her pocket. It was Tenté, screaming.

"Chiqui! Chi! Qui! Are you all right, my pigeon?"

"Yes, *loca.*"

THE FORTY-NINTH AND OTHER BOUNDARIES

Matty fell hard for Machito after cruising him in the mirror of a dive bar bathroom. He'd always been lanky and lean and was turned on by the bull stud's compact body. He'd always been reticent—a trait handed down by his Calvinist father—but was smitten when Machito flashed his easy smile. He struggled to understand Machito's heavy accent but wasn't much interested in talking anyway. They lunged for each other and it got pretty intense even as other customers came and went. They walked out of that bathroom over strains of "Rhythm Nation" practically a couple.

There was one hitch: Machito was about to overstay his tourist visa. Matty hastily arranged a trip to Punta Cana, booking three days at this all-inclusive resort promising sunbathing, Caribbean waters, and elaborate meals. Upon their return, Machito's visa would be renewed for another ninety days. That was the plan at least.

Their Dominican idyll quickly took a dark turn. On the first night, they returned to their room to find a break-in under way. The thieves jumped off the balcony and disappeared under the palmettos. They hadn't gotten away with much but had succeeded in rattling the couple. The resort manager moved them up to a higher floor. The next day at the beach, they watched as a crowd abused and beat a Haitian man, a trinket-seller who had strayed onto private property. Matty railed against the injustice, fuming at the oblivious tourists carrying on with their beach vacations. In his aggrieved state, their immigration plan was hardly front of mind when they boarded the return flight. "Let's just get the hell off this fucking island," Matty said to Machito, who'd seen worse.

Once they were instructed to form separate lines at Miami International, their plan came back into focus. From the US citizens' line, Matty's green eyes narrowed as he watched a Customs Agent go through Machito's bag. She had a round, pleasant face, a plump body, and salon waves in a short bob; she looked like a suburban mom, except for the uniform. She pulled a postcard addressed to Machito's sister from his carry-on. They hadn't found a post office, so it hadn't gotten mailed. "*Estoy trabajando en un café, esta bien.*" I'm working in a café, it's okay.

The Customs Agent's pleasant face fixed in vindictive triumph. She grinned wildly and high-fived her associate: "We got one!" Matty watched as they escorted Machito to an interrogation room; he glared back with a doomed look. He looked so small next to their wide bodies, like they could crush him with one coordinated turn. They informed Matty that Machito would be sent back to Caracas. "My government has taken my love away," Matty lamented, trying on feelings. He vowed to get him back. Sure they barely knew each other but that wasn't the point. Whatever journey they were on wasn't ending with this mean mom-lady in beige.

The immigration detention facility was a concrete bunker built on an airstrip. Relatives of the detained were gathered at the fence; one yelled a name, got an answer, so everyone else went silent. It was their only way to communicate. Matty waited his turn, then yelled "Machito! Machito!" but it just bounced off the concrete. He returned home, heartbroken. He was lamenting the situation with his friend Josh, who was dating Aimee, who was from Vancouver. "Dude, just bring him back through Canada," Josh said, like it was the most obvious solution in the world. Aimee offered to connect him with some friends, and they figured out how to get Machito into Canada without passing through U.S airspace; he'd to fly to London first, then Montreal.

Matty traveled to Montreal on Amtrak, wincing in the direction of New Paltz, where his father seethed in judgment while doing chores, then meditating on the vastness of Lake Champlain as the train chugged northward. Machito's flight had landed by the time he got to Dorval Airport; they nearly ran into each other on the crowded concourse. Machito's black eyes overflowed with tears. Matty worried about attracting attention but no one seemed to notice their reunion. They flew to Vancouver, where Matty rented a car, then headed east, where they met Aimee's three friends. They were all sons of American Vietnam-era draft dodgers and Canadian women. Strapping guys who kept their blond hair in dreadlocks, they were themselves stateless in the view of the U.S. They grew marijuana in the woods and carried it across to sell. "Machito, you're gonna walk this dry river bed. No flashlight, there's plenty of moonlight," one explained. "About three miles until it goes under a road. That's where you hide, the drainage ditch." Machito was shaking. Another gave Matty his directions: "Drive through this checkpoint, then a mile or so down the road, you'll see a guard rail on your left, that's where you pick him up." Matty freaked out at the prospect of dealing with another US border agent. The third said to Machito: "Oh! And if you see a bear, just ignore him." With this, Machito started crying and threw himself into Matty's arms. "I can no ignore bear, we no have bear in Sud America." Matty tried to be strong:

"You can do this. Just follow the river. I'll be waiting." Then the same guy said, "You guys seem stressed—wanna smoke a joint?" The smoke mellowed them out to the point they could actually laugh about their situation, until they got paranoid about forgetting their instructions. Night fell and the trio dropped them at the trailhead; Matty had to push Machito off to get him started. At the checkpoint, the agent asked Matty routine questions. It seemed to be going well until he noticed some stray pot seeds in the ashtray. He had Matty step out and went through everything looking for contraband. Of the two big suitcases in the trunk, he asked, "Why so many clothes?" Matty played the gay card: "I just never know what to pack!" That actually seemed to work.

It was a clear night; trees swayed in the breeze. Matty heard a rustle as Machito popped up from behind the guard rail. His scared eyes reflected the headlights as he scrambled to the car. "Did you see a bear?" asked Matty. "No, I run all the way," replied Machito. His heart was racing, his jeans were soggy – that river bed wasn't all that dry. "You did it!" Matty cried, as they hugged awkwardly in the bucket seats of the rental.

Matty was anxious to get to Seattle, conspicuous as they were in rural Washington state – a gay New Yorker and a brown man with fake ID. They were tearing through this hamlet when they got pulled over by a police cruiser. Matty quickly handed Machito a ball cap and said, "Pull this down over your face and pretend you're sleeping." Matty pondered the charges he'd face if caught—*Harboring a fugitive? Human trafficking?*—as an impossibly good-looking officer approached the car: black hair, blue eyes, broad chest, broad smile. He looked like a superhero but seemed mainly interested in small talk.

"Oh, you're from New York?" he asked, checking Matty's license. "I've always wanted to go…What brings you out here?"

"We're on vacation," Matty replied, adding, "just doing some hiking." This wasn't entirely untrue.

Matty held it together against his superhero charms while Machito trembled under the ball cap, tears tracking down his cheeks. Eventually the cop said, "Well, you were speeding, but I didn't have my radar gun on, so you're free to go," and flashed a superhero smile.

They drove through the night to Seattle, where they were put up by Matty's lesbian friend Gwen, who had recently relocated there after a bad break-up. "You're our Harriet Tubman!" Matty cried as they group hugged. The couple slept long hours in Gwen's guest room, hung out in coffee bars, and smoked lots of weed with her Riot Grrl clique. Walking around the Capitol Hill area, they felt safe and free for the first time since that fateful day with the mean mom-lady. They eventually booked a flight back to New York, via Houston.

◆

Things fell apart soon after their "Canadian vacation," as they referred to their trip. Their friends knew enough not to ask too many questions about Machito's unexpected return. They were happy for them, although Matty and Machito were locked in unbreakable dysfunction. They couldn't help but remind each other of their respective trauma. *Your stupid plan! That stupid postcard!* Machito went back to his job at the café while Matty stumbled through his days in a stoned haze, tracing the jagged spiral of his lover's journey on an atlas:

Caracas > London > Montreal > Vancouver > Seattle > Houston

At a celebratory dinner, Josh asked Matty, "I don't get it, man. You got him back. So why are you unhappy?" Matty could only muster a dazed grimace. Aimee whispered into Josh's ear: "He's still detained at the forty-ninth, at least emotionally." Matty wasn't supposed to hear her poetic assessment. Josh and Aimee were his border-crossing enablers, his only confidantes. Their reaction punctured his misery.

He resolved to clear his mind and talk to Machito. They still really didn't know each other that well. He put the atlas back on the bookshelf and tapered himself off of his daily pot habit. On his way home from a fresh haircut, summoning this new resolve in the spring air, he spotted Machito and one of his co-workers from the café loading Machito's big suitcase into a taxi. His last words to Matty—which he had memorized off of a tea tin—were perfectly enunciated: "No boundary stops the heart of a person that loves."

PART II: VECTORS

CHOKE A HORSE

"What's the charge?" Nick demanded as the cop handcuffed him.

"Indecent exposure," the cop replied.

"Nothing was exposed until you came along with your flashlights."

Once his righteous indignation wore off and the cell door locked, a current of relief soothed Nick's emotional disorder. He'd been transported by van to a renovated facility. From the outside, it had the woodsy charm of an Adirondack lodge, while the interior was gray and efficient. The patrol had come upon Nick not far from the Rustic Shelter; his jeans were pulled down and he was getting fucked. His trick had shown amazing reflexes and dashed off through the thicket in the direction of the Gill. One of the cops chased after him but soon gave up and turned his attention on Nick. The ambush in that dense thicket came as a complete surprise; now, with two cops bearing down on him, he went silent. This was not the encounter with law enforcement he'd been dreading of late, since he'd tied up Mr. Smart and helped himself to a roll of money in his safe.

It was the most cash he'd ever handled, a roll of hundreds that turned in on itself like a serpent eating its tail, engorged with value. There was some thin blood drying on it—which had spurted from Mr. Smart's nose when he'd punched him—and a couple of cracked rubber bands barely doing the job of holding it together. Nick had no idea Mr. Smart kept gangster rolls in his safe. He was only vaguely aware of its existence. "I had those boys carve back all the walls to make room for my bed," he'd boasted of his demands on his hunky construction crew. "They found a niche for the safe, too." Nick had seen through the doorway that it was hidden behind one of the Jacobean nightstands, and stuffed with good watches, yellowed stock certificates, and a stash of photos of him pouting in front of European palaces.

The punch culminated Nick's leaving Mr. Smart for what he told himself was the last time; but he'd told himself that many times before. There was that period when he'd checked out and sniffed heroin for a winter. Once he ran out of money and his buddy with the score went to rehab, he went back. Nick cleaned up after a month and Mr. Smart approved of his newly-thin build, as if his dope stint was a diet camp for alcohol bloat. "He's always so forgiving of me," Nick would say of his return, but it was more about the money than some fiction of absolution. Still, he was convinced that his last stunt would have Mr. Smart calling the police.

A movie scene flashed into his head in which a mob underling handles a similar roll, squeezes it a couple of times, and declares it "thick enough to choke a horse." The turn of phrase startled him once he found himself handling such a roll: was he its intended horse?

He'd been crossing through the Ramble by night for years, as Mr. Smart lived on the East Side and he lived on the West. He navigated its paths by moonlight, nodding to a few familiar huddles of men. Sometimes ambling through its shabby splendor was the only way to shake off Mr. Smart's fixated gaze. They'd drink at crossed purposes: Mr. Smart wanted to get Nick incapacitated enough to fall into bed with him, and Nick wanted Mr. Smart to pass out so he could take the money and go home.

Nick couldn't recall the factors that made him desperate enough to tie Mr. Smart to one of his throne-like Gothic Revival chairs, with peacock blue flocked velvet upholstery. He used Mr. Smart's bespoke neckties to bind his wrists to the hand-carved wooden arms and his ankles to the gilt legs. The arms had upholstered sections too, one now stained with blood. Something about seeing this aristocratic British man tied to his throne with his own silk had soothed him, like the synchronized click of jail door magnets on multiple strike plates. *Behold my colonizer!* He laughed maniacally at the thought.

He didn't really need the money, in retrospect. He wasn't about to get thrown out of his apartment; his dealer was paid. Maybe he had a credit card bill hanging over him, but who didn't? Thanks to his years-long relationship with Mr. Smart, he'd been living the life of a pampered pretty boy, one who knew to keep the edges just rough enough. What he really sought was to re-assert some dominance over his now-withholding sugar daddy.

He'd met Mr. Smart when he was a sophomore in college studying architecture. He was Mr. Smart's romantic ideal: a sullen Italian youth, even if he was Bensonhurst Italian. Mr. Smart embraced the strain of English Romanticism that glorified Italy for its sublime nature, splendid ruins, and sensuous people. He was a society decorator with a certain cachet in the business and an impressive roster of past clients: old-money grand dames, nouveau riche strivers, socialites. His style was lifted off the British aristocracy; colors and patterns evoking the glories of nature, careful arrangements of coveted objects acquired from the farthest reaches of the Empire, projecting a veneer of status.

One night at dinner in a posh restaurant, Mr. Smart proposed they enter an arrangement: dinner dates and evenings together in exchange for a weekly stipend. Nick made a counter offer: he would be the draftsman for his decoration projects. They started out on his terms, and wound up on Mr. Smart's. As his decor business stalled, his drinking escalated, and Nick's role transitioned from draftsman to cocktail companion. Where once he saw himself as an observer of the habits of this insular tribe—conducting an anthropology of the Upper East Side—he lately felt like a pampered pet around this social set.

On the nights Nick won the race he'd cross Central Park to get home. Sometimes he took a taxi, sometimes the cross-town bus. When he wasn't too swervy from drink he'd walk. Although sensationalist news stories of wilding youth gangs didn't track with his experience, it was still a fraught crossing: he was usually dressed up in a suit, at least half-drunk, and carrying cash. It was on those nights that Nick discovered the gay cruising scene in the Ramble, the 'wild garden' landscape architect Olmstead had crafted out of Manhattan woodlands. The area attracted sexually adventurous gay men of all ages and skin tones. By day, they shared the territory with binocular-sporting bird watchers; they took over at night. Nick felt like a man among men in the Ramble, not kept.

Tying Mr. Smart down and roughing him up seemed like his best and last option. Mr. Smart had become withdrawn and morose as his health declined, the result of his excessive drinking. What was worse, he'd become cheap, doling out what was once a weekly stipend every nine days, now ten, now attaching new conditions. He'd made a decision he was going to spend his days drinking in his accustomed manner, and calculated that his remaining money was adequate to finance that plan. As his bank account dwindled, he began to look upon his aged-out, bloated kept boy as an investment with diminishing returns.

The night of his arrest, Nick had been startled awake by a rustling noise out on the fire escape. The windows were open for a cross-breeze to the airshaft. His apartment had been broken into before, but never when he was home. Still, he immediately checked to see if the roll of bills was still there. He couldn't bring himself to deposit it, and had only spent the bloody outer bill on a quarter. The roll and the smoke were there under the covers at the foot of the bed but Nick couldn't get back to sleep. He locked the windows and hid the roll of bills behind the radiator. Walking into the dark cool of the park, he cleared a path through the wreckage of his decade-long entanglement.

If Mr. Smart had lost interest, so had Nick. He was a roached-out stoner by then. He'd started getting high just so he could bear to show up and drink with Mr. Smart. For a time, pot kept him affable enough to sit through those long nights, to play the outré charmer for his society friends. But the payback was due. He was angry, blaming Mr. Smart for his own dysfunction and all those wasted years. All the tools he could have used to finesse the situation were blunted. What he really needed was to punch through the crossfire-riddled haze. Compounding the dissociative effects of their alcohol use and Nick's drug habit was Mr. Smart's increasing reliance on prescriptions. They were hardly ever on the same frequency any more. A question hung over their every night: Which would prove more resilient, Mr. Smart's romantic fixation or Nick's greed?

Nick got to the rustic shelter and lit up a joint; a few men stalked the perimeter. A wiry *chulo* ambled right up to him and pursed his full lips. Nick held the joint for him to draw on, and the guy grabbed him from behind the neck and shotgunned the smoke back into his mouth. It was a wordless assertion of desire and it worked on Nick, who was tired of talking anyway. The stranger's skin glowed under the dim light as he led Nick through the thicket; he pinned Nick against a tree trunk and groped him roughly.

Once Nick had taken satisfaction from seeing his colonizer bound and gagged, he was at a loss, and a fury of unspoken resentments took over. He did what he'd dared himself to do because he couldn't think of anything else; he punched Mr. Smart in the face. Mr. Smart's dental bridge flew out of his mouth, and blood spurted from his nose. His blood was thin and hardly clotted anymore, so it just poured out watery red in a steady stream. After landing the punch, Nick broke down at his feet. "I can't do this anymore," he sobbed. He eventually untied Mr. Smart, who retrieved his bridge and stuffed a silk handkerchief in his nostril, muttering, "I understand, I quite understand," but not much more.

Indecent exposure. The charge stung more than his trick's hasty pull-out, because Nick always thought his ass was decent, even better. He breathed through panic as he anticipated all the other charges he was convinced they'd soon add: kidnapping, assault, robbery. An uninvited wave of compassion for drunken, lovelorn Mr. Smart coursed through his system. "Maybe I'd finally given him the rough scene he always wanted but didn't know how to ask for," Nick muttered as he stared past the bars to the clerestory, fixating on a branch gently scraping the glass on that stifling summer night. "Oh, now you wanna talk," the arresting cop said sarcastically, as he swiveled in his office chair, lifted his powerful body, flashlights and handcuffs jangling at his hips, and followed his partner back out into the Ramble.

JESUS YEAR

Marta from housekeeping knocked on the door of room 401 and heard a muffled groan. "*O, Dios*," she muttered as she opened the door cautiously, remembering all the other inopportune encounters with hotel guests. Her mind indexed each lurid scenario—every drunk wallowing in his own filth, every old man with a lingerie girl half his age. It was a catalog of base horrors she'd assembled in her time working in hotels and it impacted how she thought about Americans. It was almost enough to make her long for the mushroom farm. They were stern but decent people. *Why were the guests incapable of using the 'do not disturb' placards?* She asked herself as she entered the room.

She found the registered guest, a mister Chris Tolliver, in one of the hotel's plush bathrobes, slumped against the headboard. His wrists were tied to the wall sconces on either side of the bed with robe sashes. His dark curls were matted to his head with sweat, and his green irises stood out against the pink of his bloodshot sclera like inverted watermelons. The sconces were illuminated while the robe was wide open, doing little to conceal his hairy nakedness; he had what looked like a pair of briefs stuffed into his mouth. Marta rolled her eyes and crossed herself before springing into action.

She held up his arm to put some slack in the sash, and released the slip knot at his wrist. "Sir, are you alright? Were you robbed?" she asked as she removed the briefs with a gloved hand.

"A little," he replied incoherently, stretching his jaw.

On the television, a History Channel program was airing, in which the Norwegian explorer Thor Heyerdahl explained his theory of trans-atlantic trade between South America and North Africa, via the Canary Current, over a reenactment. The narrator advanced the tale breathlessly, "World sensation, the navigator of the Kon-Tiki, Thor Heyerdahl, built papyrus rafts in the manner seen is Egyptian sepulchral paintings from the fifth century."

Chris Tolliver stretched his freed arm, detecting the aches beneath the numbness.

"He christened the vessel Ra, the ancient Egyptians' name for the sun," the narrator continued. Traders in reed boats had navigated the current, and that's how, Mister Heyerdahl speculated, Egyptian mummies buried inside the pyramids were found to have traces of cocaine.

"See? My shit is pure. I'm like the pharaohs," Chris said to Marta, who turned off the television.

In the last year, Chris had come into a sizable inheritance, though not from a family member. Milo Smart was a British-born decorator of a certain renown, a style guru for Manhattan's Upper East Side. He'd hired Chris when he was a young design student to draft his interior projects for his affluent clientele. Over a year of working closely with his handsome young disciple, Milo had become smitten. Chris had found himself spending more and more of his time at restaurant tables rather than the drafting table; Milo was a man of appetites and appearances, so he liked having Chris along as a companion at all the posh eateries frequented by his crowd. He revealed his feelings over dinner at Chanterelle, Chris' favorite.

"I doubt you could love an old wreck like me, but perhaps you can find..." Milo asked, tracing figures with his hand.

"Some affection?" Chris finished his thought. Milo smiled.

◆

Last summer, Milo was on a seaplane to Sag Harbor to see the new home of a client when the craft lost power and crash landed in the bay short of the dock. The pilot and the other passengers were rescued with some injuries, but Milo alone had prematurely removed his seatbelt and had been thrown forward upon impact, sustaining a fatal blow to the head. His funeral was the society neck-craning spectacular of the season. Milo's long-suffering ex-lover—the executor of his will—surprised Chris with news of his inheritance. "He was really quite fond of you, young man," he said, and Chris was genuinely moved. "Beyond his absurd infatuation," he added caustically.

Chris had checked into the Hotel Bethlehem with a bag full of money. It was one of those ordinary white plastic bags given to shoppers at stores all over the city, printed with the I ♥ NY logo. He'd booked a limo to take him and some friends to the casino, which was built on the grounds of the town's namesake steel mill, now abandoned. The buzz of the gaming floor in that setting brought to his mind maggots swarming an animal carcass.

"You're the lucky one here, Chris, try the blackjack table," Efgeny said.

He'd met all of them on a night out some weeks ago and couldn't remember any of their names. He suspected Efgeny, a lean hipster boy with dark features, was some kind of hacker. He knew how to count cards so all night he sat behind Chris, whispering into his ear what to bet, whether or not to take a card. Chris won a small fortune and split it with him. They drank martinis until they got thrown out, and on the way out, the crew yelled Chris' praises to anyone they came upon.

After that terrific drinking marathon, he'd sent his friends back to New York in the waiting limo without him. He'd come to loathe their fawning. The hotel receptionist looked askance at his lack of luggage, so he pulled a twenty out of the bag and managed a smile. In the year since receiving the check from the lawyer, Chris had burned through much of his gay inheritance. What was in the bag was all that was left of it, though Chris was now perplexed to find that bag weighed more than when he'd left New York. He didn't remember winning.

"These sconces get freaking hot. Crucified! Well, it's the end of my Jesus year, so it's the look," he said to Marta, only a bit more coherently.

Marta had suffered drunkenness and she had suffered depravity but she had never been party to this sort of blasphemy. She summoned her composure and crossed to the other side of the bed as he seemed incapable of helping himself out of his bondage. "Don't flatter yourself, mister," Marta said as untied his other wrist. "I don't see any nails," she remarked.

"Ugh, they went into my head instead of my hands, dear," replied Chris, rubbing his temples with his free hand. "But that's where I do all my laying and running anyway," he added.

Marta gave Chris a stern look and shook her head, as she worked on his still-bound wrist. Once he was free, he went in for a hug, but Marta backed him off. "Could you..." asked Marta, indicating his nakedness, and to her dismay, he put on the soggy briefs.

She said nails. Chris Tolliver had whispered about nails to himself over and again, whenever pondering Jesus on the back wall. There was this whispered taunt and it had justified years of bad choices. *Don't worry*, his inner voice would say, *you'll be nailed up like Jesus by the time you're thirty-three.* This intonation had been on infinite repeat since he was an adolescent. Though the Church of his youth had weak currents of Seventies Liberation Theology running through it—he could still remember the words to *Michael, Row the Boat Ashore*, and Sister Regina's fervent guitar lead—the hierarchy was still entrenched in Old-World damnation. This was confusing, so one day when a fuse blew and the lights went out, Chris walked out of catechism. He haughtily announced to his parents he wouldn't be going back. It was then, in a spasm of narcissistic guilt, that the internal whisper campaign started.

"How very Catholic," his therapist had remarked. The prediction had hardened like a stalactite into fatalistic certainty over years of repetition.

In college, Chris had adopted the pose of a dissolute. He'd latched on to Milo Smart, initially as entrée into the uptown scene, and wound up his companion. Milo was a lover of all things Italian: villas, statues, food, men. Milo nourished his romantic obsession for Chris with elaborate meals and wine. Chris went all over the city with the man—who himself looked like the Pope, with his aristocratic jowls, his dainty shoes, his fine blonde hair, his large, imposing body enrobed in finery.

Shortly before his death, Milo took Chris on a tour of Southern Italy, a return to Chris' homeland, and Milo's Romantic idyll. They visited royal palaces, fabulous gardens, and splendid ruins—settings in which he felt Chris belonged. They spent a day at the baroque Reggia di Caserta, constructed in the Eighteenth century for the Bourbon King of Naples. Touring the English Garden, a naturalistic paradise with Vesuvius hovering in the distance, was Milo's main objective. He took a photo of Chris in the garden, with the dormant volcano in the background. Chris felt like an exiled prince restored to the throne.

Milo expected him to drink wine along with him in the suits he had made for him. Their nights out were a race to the bottom. Chris wanted him to pass out so he could take a taxi home, and Milo wanted to get him drunk enough to fall into bed with him. He responded to Milo's romantic overtures with increasing cruelty—until one night, when Milo finally wore him down. Milo threw himself on his belly and just sort of held himself there, like a walrus bull warming himself on a rock and Chris was his sun. *Don't worry*, Chris' inner voice repeated, allaying his shame. *You'll be nailed up soon.*

After Milo's death, Chris embarked on his thirties with an unexpected inheritance. Pope Milo was dead and his prince was unleashed. Chris been regularly getting high just to be able to put up with the obsessed old man. He found that he had nurtured his own addiction which was now unleashed, too. Once he came into all that money, he was buying bags of mind-numbing sativa, these excellent strains, from a dealer who lived in his new building. He'd become such a lethargic stoner that he needed some kind of stimulant.

He'd never used cocaine up until then. It was provided by an ex-boyfriend from Venezuela who spoke English with an accent only Chris seemed to comprehend, but had an excellent supplier. His compulsion had escalated to the point where he'd been found by Marta in the hotel room, his pretty mouth stuffed with his own undies, his thoughts misfiring. His neural network was fried; what crossed his synapses was a spiky tangle. "My very own crown of thorns," Chris said, bringing his hands up to his head.

Marta noticed a cut on his torso, just under his right nipple. The hairy patch below his pectorals was matted with blood. She almost swooned when she realized what it was—she'd always been squeamish in that way, ever since she was made to help her father when he killed the chickens. She steadied herself and made her way over to the house phone.

"Please don't tell anyone—I'm all right," Chris begged. The prospect of medical attention had a sobering effect.

Marta hesitated, and then found some courage.

"Tell me what the hell happened here," she demanded, one hand on the handset.

"Well, uh…what's your name? I can't read your tag," he said, squinting.

"Marta."

"Thank you for untying me, Marta," he said.

"Of course."

"I'm Chris. Nice to meet you. You know, the church considers me fallen away. Doesn't that sound pleasant?"

Marta picked up the handset again.

"Okay! I picked up some rough trade online. He worked me over."

Marta absorbed this new information and walked away from the phone. She went over to her cart and retrieved a first aid kit. She was going to just hand him the supplies, but he was so obviously useless that she ended up cleaning and dressing his wound, holding back her revulsion.

"Marta, will you help me get back at him?"

"I don't think that's a good idea. I have to clean all these rooms…" she replied, tapping her clipboard.

"I just want to lure him back to the hotel…"

"Why would he come back here?"

"Trust me, he'll come back. Could you just let me into a different room?"

"Oh, no, I cannot do that. I will lose my job."

"An empty room, one you haven't cleaned yet. Please?" He scrambled to find some twenties, but before he could find any saw that he'd already convinced her. Despite his impaired state, Chris was a charmer.

Chris fabricated a new profile on Grindr. He used one of Milo's old photos and made up a compelling back story for him. His catfish profile was an old-money Philadelphian from Rittenhouse Square who had won big at the casino over the weekend and had decided to sleep in and spend an extra day at the hotel. He approached Lance, the guy from last night. Lance quickly agreed to meet in a room on the seventh floor.

The room Marta let him use for the confrontation was a suite, sought after for its view of the Bethlehem Star—an illuminated display set on tall scaffolding in the nearby woods. Chris hid in the bedroom closet; he didn't want Lance to catch sight of him. There was a mirror over the desk and he had worked out the sight lines. Marta stalled Lance, giving him the impression that she'd been called in to freshen up the living room.

Listening through the louvered closet door reminded Chris of his first confession. He'd crossed himself like they taught him in catechism as he entered the confessional and said the *Bless me father for I have sinned* line and waited expectantly.

When the priest whispered, "Well son, tell me your sins," young Chris was appalled. Maybe he hadn't been paying attention, but he expected that the priest would already know his sins. He must be able to divine them through the stamped metal screen, he reasoned. What was the magic in telling? Why did they even bother with this ornate booth? He couldn't even think of any good sins, so if the priest couldn't tell him what was wrong, what good was he?

"I...I don't think that's any of your business," Chris had blurted out.

The priest sighed. "Go back to Sister Regina, ask her to explain Holy Confession, son..." Chris walked out of the booth and straight home in sullen indignation. It was his first confession and his last. His full renunciation of the faith came soon after.

Marta was surprised by Lance's appearance; he was a nice-looking young man dressed in sweatpants and clean sneakers and carrying a backpack. He was friendly and treated her kindly. Unbeknownst to Marta, Lance was one of the Lehigh Valley's most popular escorts. He marketed himself as a college boy offering the full boyfriend experience and occasionally took calls in Philadelphia and New York. He really was a college student—though not at Lehigh University as his sweatpants suggested. He attended a nearby community college and was in his last semester of a degree in Environmental Science. He was finishing up a research project about the impact of hydraulic fracturing of Marcellus Shale on the Valley. He paid his own tuition and even bought his mom gas cards with the money he made escorting. Chris had been drawn in by Lance's concise profile on Backpage:

Lehigh Valley college stud, 24, 5'11, thick. Athletic lean build. Fetish friendly. Outcalls only. "Sublime natures are seldom clean." Lance.

All Marta knew was that Lance didn't seem like some desperado who would tie a man up and rob him. She wondered why such a composed young man would even want to be around Chris. She had a weakness for blonde men despite herself. Once Lance was sitting down and Marta had gotten a good look at him, Chris emerged from the bedroom. He'd cleaned himself up and dressed in last night's crumpled clothes, though there was still an emptiness in his eyes. Lance caught sight of him and said, "Oh no, not you again," and hustled towards the door, whereupon Marta blocked it with her cart.

"Please, Lance, I just want to say sorry about last night," said Chris.

Marta gave a confused look.

"Let him go, if he wants," Chris said to Marta. "He didn't rob me. It was just a scene gone wrong."

"No, I didn't rob anyone," Lance said to Marta, "I was paid for an hour, and the session went over. Mainly because he wouldn't stop talking." He made the yapping hand gesture, and Marta found herself sympathizing. Then turning to Chris, he said, "Sorry I left you like that— you just annoyed the balls off of me."

"So explain this—how did he get stabbed?" asked Marta.

"He tripped over his pants and landed on a bottle opener," replied Lance.

"Oh, right," Chris said, remembering.

"I tried to help him clean it up, but he wouldn't let me," Lance added.

Marta scowled at Chris. "I should have known better…"

"I'm sorry, really. I was strung out. I was tripping on some fractured burial myths. Jesus, the pharaohs, all scramble," said Chris. "There are too many stories in my head," he pleaded. Then he turned to Lance: "I just wanted you to know I'm sorry. I'll make it up to you, okay? If you'll see me again—a nice, normal date. I mean, I'll give you your full rate, of course. We'll have dinner on the terrace. No bondage, no blow."

His kink went back to his childhood; a session always brought him back to his first time tied up. It was his older brother and the kid next door, who had a sadistic streak. They didn't like playing with him, but when they deigned to include him, it was only for one game: Batman and Robin. Chris was always Robin, because his brother was always Batman. The next door kid was one of the villains; he was a comic book collector, always pulling out the obscure ones. That day, he announced, "I call Deathstroke," and enlisted a cricket mallet as his weapon.

Playing Robin meant getting ambushed by the villain—being wrestled to the ground while avoiding a fatal blow from the cricket mallet. Deathstroke tied him to the wooden fence between their yards with some bungee cords. Robin watched the battle between his captor and Batman for the cricket mallet, as the fencepost dug into his back. At least he was included. He was even being fought over. He enjoyed being pained and restrained—or at least the way it blanked out all the emotional disorder. After a while, the tedium of the battle set in, his body ached, and he slouched, still bound to the fencepost. His muscles strained against the tightening cords while an erection pushed against his shorts. The boys' fight spilled into the front yard and he was left alone for a time. Dusk settled. It should have been frightening but it registered as serene order. He knew he'd eventually be saved just like they kept trying to tell him in catechism.

"Okay, sure," said Lance, handing Chris his card. "But keep it cute."

Chris kissed Lance then crumbled into his embrace. The soapy scent of Lance's skin stirred a reckoning and he shuddered. The formative myth of the Catholic faith had ensnared him in its thorny, long-haired clutches, though he'd run from it for years ever since walking out of that confessional. He was mortally embarrassed about enlisting Lance in his jacked-up reenactment. "God, how I've rambled," Chris mumbled into Lance's neck, sobbing. Now the tears flowed after years of drought. It was the one story he'd sold himself on through years of repetition and it had run his life.

Lance took his head in his hands and said, "Get it together, man," then walked out the door.

Chris, left hulking towards an absent body in the Star Suite, was engulfed in waves of remorse. He'd bent time, space, geography, history, social order, reason, morality, and judgment to fit a bogus myth. He was thirty-four and wasn't quite dead, just really fucking impaired. Marta looked on with pity.

Chris was seized with panic, suddenly aware that his timeline was not so predetermined. He scrawled a note on the hotel stationery and handed it to Marta. "Safe," he said to her with emphasis. Then he hugged her, and she let him this time, though a little stiffly. He walked out of the suite and down into the lobby, past a tour group which was gathered to peek in on the Presidential Suite, where several American presidents had rested their heads after touring the Lehigh Valley. He walked out of the stately building as the guide started on his spiel about Eisenhower and Kennedy, to make everyone happy. He walked east on Pembroke and kept walking–through Easton, through Long Valley.

Shortly after crossing into New Jersey, he stopped at a gas station for headache pills and a cola, then continued his hike through Morristown, through South Mountain State Park, where he heard but did not see a waterfall, and through the summer night. He arrived at the bank of the Hudson River in Jersey City in the late morning and boarded a ferry at Paulus Hook. Thankfully he still had his sunglasses. Upon landing on Manhattan he walked up Broadway to his apartment. The doorman greeted him with a robust "Good Morning, Mister Tolliver," then as soon as Chris was in the elevator, called the super to gossip.

The painting over his tufted couch was a depiction of Jesus after the medieval style, coasting out of his crumpled body towards heaven. It was a surprise gift from Milo on their trip to Italy; they'd come across it while hunting for antiques in the Borgo Parioli. After Chris admired the depiction of the heavenly light, Milo had circled back and arranged to buy it. Chris shed his filthy clothes, drew the blinds, and lined up some water bottles on the coffee table. Then he sprawled on the couch and slept for three days.

Back at the Hotel Bethlehem, Marta opened the note Chris had written her, which read: 'He is not here. He has risen.' She rolled her cart into the elevator and headed back down to room 401. She opened a window to freshen the air—there was an acrid chemical odor under the muskiness. She resumed her work. When she was finished vacuuming the carpet, she turned on the television for her novela. While she listened to Teresa, the most powerful *narcotraficante* in all of Mexico, confront the handsome police informant, she polished the marble and the nickel fittings in the bathroom. She cleaned the mirrors. She changed the sheets, the towels, and the bath robes, lugging all the soiled items to the laundry cart. She restocked the soaps and lotions. The actor who played the informant reminded her of her father; she winced involuntarily when he spoke his lines.

She stuck Chris Tolliver's note in the clipboard over her work detail, which indicated she was readying the room for the Valastros. She recognized the name; they were regular visitors, driving into town for a hospitality industry conference. She recognized the verse too, a regular visitor to her spiritual house, but had to check the bible in the nightstand to find it, in the Gospel of Matthew. Once she had emptied the garbage pails and reset the air controls, she went over to the room safe and tried the combination 2-8-6. It opened for her with a blink of the indicator light and inside was the bag full of money.

WORKER NAME

He first came off as a fast-talking bullshitter, until his voice shifted from loud cockiness to a nearly incomprehensible mumble. He could talk but couldn't seem to say what he wanted. These red flags prompted the "Have you been partying?" screening question, to which he answered, "Just a little smoke." Nico assumed he was referring to marijuana. While other drugs are smoked, hash is too exotic to not mention, dope or meth are not "just" drugs, and opium... Well, if this dude on East Seventh was sitting on a floor cushion smoking opium, Nico would just chuck his recovery and join him there forever.

"Well, as long as you stick to smoke. If you level up to the hard stuff, I'm out," Nico said.

"Totally, got it. We're cool."

"We'll see."

He lived close by so if it was a bad scene, Nico could just split, no loss.

"So what's your name?" he asked, not offering his.

"Dom." This wasn't the name he usually gave. He'd just read it off the cigar box that held his savings. He felt a need to protect himself.

"Short for Dominick?"

"Sure," Nico replied.

"And you live around here?"

He's trying to pin me down, Nico thought. "I wish, I'm house-sitting for a friend."

"Oh, right on..."

Even through the wild swings between cockiness and incomprehensible torpor, Nico detected a Cali dude cadence. He kept assuring Nico that he had money as if this were a stand-in for knowing what he wanted and being able to ask for it.

It was a yuppified East Village tenement flat with exposed brick and an updated kitchen. Nico detected a biting odor lurking beneath the clouds of cannabis smoke. In person, he came off even more Cali dude, with his board shorts, flip-flops, and hoodie getup, his dirty blond hair, his stubble, his blissed-out smile. He seemed unable to focus his attention for very long, and hyperactively bopped to Green Day playing on his iPod.

Nico relaxed a bit—until he noticed a skinny kid huddling in the corner. Cali dude hadn't said anything about another guy. He was a lean hipster boy with dark features. *Damn, just my type*, Nico thought to himself. The kid looked a little gray. Nico introduced himself, as Dom.

"Efgeny," he replied, with a soft handshake.

"What's this guy's deal?" Nico asked.

"This crazy man. I not understand what he want from me," he replied in a heavy Bulgarian accent.

Cali dude pulled out an earbud and yelled over, "Just ignore him, he's useless."

Efgeny shook his head and said, "I feel not so good. Better not to try what he's smoking."

"What's he smoking?" Nico asked.

"I think crack," he replied.

"What the hell? This bro motherfucker is smoking crack?" Nico hadn't even considered this possibility, it was such a throwback. His outburst got Cali dude's attention over the music again.

"He was just leaving," Cali dude said of Efgeny, who rolled his eyes hard.

Since when is crack 'just a little smoke?' Nico circled back to their phone call. He sniffed the air and found it lingering, harsh, sweet, burnt plastic mixed with wet ink. Nico had on his hands a yuppie on crack with a sick Eastern European hustler in tow. Growing up in the Eighties he'd watched as whole blocks of his neighborhood turn into armed outposts over that fugitive high. He'd never encountered casual crack use, only that all-consuming, destructive compulsion. "Rock will fuck your mother in front of you," was how his upstairs neighbor had once put it.

Cali dude disparaged Efgeny some more; something about not being able to get the job done. Nico was really pissed at him for giving the kid crack. This was a hostage situation above a store of dynamite. Cali dude downplayed by saying things like, "I'm totally cool" and "I have my own business, make good money." To prove his point, he showed Nico his checking account balance: thirty-eight thousand dollars. "See?" asked Cali dude, as he flashed a crumpled ATM receipt.

Nico told Cali dude he was uncomfortable with the scene but Cali dude pleaded; a boyish charm emerged from behind his desperation. Nico asked him straight out: "What do you want?" Cali dude hemmed and hawed in barely intelligible bro-speak. Nico finally came to understand—by inference and hand gestures—that Cali dude wanted to take a hit off his pipe, then just when the rush hit, Nico was to forcibly fuck him.

Nico really wanted to bail but was counting the time already invested; plus the color had come back to Efgeny's handsome face. There was the money, too; Cali dude would be soon relieved of it anyway, he figured. He agreed to do what he wanted, on the condition that Cali dude go to the ATM up front. He did not want to go outside, but Nico persuaded him. The trio went downstairs, but halfway up the block, Cali dude ran home in a panic. Nico turned to Efgeny and said "Let's go," and took him back to his place.

"Did he pay you anything?" asked Nico. His phone rang with multiple calls from Cali dude, which he ignored.

"No, but I got this," and flashed Cali dude's iPod.

"You stole his iPod?" Nico asked, smiling.

"No, I not steal! He offer it as collateral." It sounded like something that wheedling bullshitter would say. Efgeny was feeling better. "Today my birthday, at least iPod is present," he said.

Efgeny had hooded eyes, with expressions fluctuating between country innocence and depraved hedonist. He'd come to the U.S. with work visa job at a software company, which he'd found boring. With thick meat between his legs he'd decided to hustle instead. He'd spend his take on clothes, electronics, and partying with his hipster friends.

"Well, since it's your birthday, I'll let you fuck me," Nico said with a wink, and afterwards he ordered them steak dinners and chocolate cake from the Latin restaurant around the corner.

Weeks later, Cali dude contacted Nico, desperate for his iPod. He apologized for being all sketchy. He was paranoid that he was going to get robbed. *Yea, Cali dude, maybe you shouldn't be flashing your ATM receipts around*, he thought.

Instead he simply said, "Crack will do that, bro."

"Yea, Dom, I mean…" Cali dude hedged, and Nico jumped in:

"You need to get off that shit before your bank account circles the drain."

Cali dude fell silent, possibly for the first time in years.

Nico arranged a swap: the iPod for Efgeny's money. He did what Cali dude wanted, for which Cali dude paid double. It was no easy feat wrestling him to the ground mid-rush, avoiding the smoke cloud and the pipe, bending him over, pinning him down, and breaking open his clenched, yuppie-on-crack ass. Cali dude howled at the first hint of penetration, so Nico gave him a hard slap in the face as he pushed in. He then fell into a glazed stupor. Nico wasn't into the scene at all, not even for a hate-fuck vibe. It was just annoying.

After a follow-up visit to give Efgeny his money, Nico had closed the case of the cracked-out Cali dude and was focusing on his regulars. At least they were known quantities. Some time later, he was walking up Second Avenue, chatting with a sober buddy, when he saw Cali dude lingering outside of his recovery program meeting. Judging from his healthy glow and the light in his eyes, he'd kicked the crack. Nico watched him glad-hand other sober people as they formed squashed little circles along the sidewalk. Beside some residual tics, he was thriving, a happy, light-filled bro, prompting Nico to wonder if he'd twelve-stepped him with his cock.

"Dom! Dom!" Cali dude spotted him and ran over.

Nico's buddy gave him a puzzled look; Nico just shrugged.

"Oh hey, man."

You saved my life, bro," said Cali dude, hugging him.

Eh, Nico thought to himself. He'd done what he needed to protect himself from a sketchy john.

"I can't forget what you said, Dom," he said, rocking Nico's stiff body to and fro.

Nico couldn't remember anything he'd said along those lines; he'd even forgotten he'd used another name. He'd taken his regular worker name, Nico, the one he advertised, from his father, since he wasn't using it any more. It was short and distinct, and appealed to his johns. They loved to say it, elongating the O sound. Some of them shouted it, too. It telegraphed the fantasy he was selling, the "guido stud dream date," as one of his reviewers had once put it. *Pimping out your heritage, that's the American way*, he reasoned, whenever memories of his father intruded on his solitude.

Standing in his buddy's searching gaze, Nico didn't want to explain why this eager newcomer was calling him that name, that fiction on top of a fiction, but his soft underbelly felt exposed. *Now this dude knows I'm a sober hustler*, Nico thought. He'd managed to keep those two circles out of forming a Venn diagram up until now. He was pleased about Cali dude's transformation, but he was more shaken now than when he'd been locked in the apartment with him, the glass pipe, and the ashen Bulgarian boy. He caught his breath, disengaged from the hug, and gave Cali dude a big smile.

"Ah, you know, practice these principles in *all* your affairs."

RAUNCH DADDY

January 21st. Scene from a break-up:

"Just go, Nick. You're too emotionally unavailable."

"This is as available as I get," I pleaded. He slammed the door shut.

This year has been trouble on trouble already. First I got laid off due to the recession, then my boyfriend kicked me out with this final review. I found a sublet a few blocks away. All my savings went to the deposit and upfront rent and I feel like a lurker in my former life. See? I have feelings.

Facing uncertainty and loneliness, Nick went on a fitness kick. He shed his relationship weight running around Tompkins Square Park, waiting his turn to do pull-ups in the exercise yard. After seeing results from the combined effects of regular workouts and his newly austere diet, he began cruising AOL's gay chat rooms. He enjoyed the attention he received in the chat rooms. Turning thirty had been marked by a lively dinner with friends at the fanciest Indian restaurant on Sixth Street, followed by a cake with sparklers arranged by his now ex. Thirty-one found him alone in a barren studio perched at his iMac chasing freelance work by day and validation by night. Thankfully his upstairs neighbor didn't know enough to password-protect her wifi signal.

HornyJohnUWS: *Come uptown. I'll make it worth your while.*

NickofTime: *Thanks, John but I'm gonna pass.*
HornyJohnUWS: *R U $ure?*

February 29th. Leap year, huh? I'm not getting enough freelance work, but at least I look good lol. I've been hitting the M4M chat rooms and it's good to know I can still pull trade after getting thrown out! This one chat room regular I've turned down repeatedly—mostly because he lives on the Upper West Side—does not quit. After yet another rejection, he offered me money. I don't see anything wrong with it. Gigs are scarce right now, and the jobs I've invoiced are taking forever to pay.

Nick showered, dressed, and caught the train to the West Side line. John answered the door and initiated some small talk. He was an antiques dealer with a lover, a dog, and a house in New Hope. He had a really hairy ass crack, and tensed up at the faintest hint of penetration, but Nick persevered, like a trailblazer through dense jungle. John was audibly delighted.

They hadn't really discussed a dollar amount. As he was getting dressed, John said, "You're as good as any hustler I've ever hired, so you get the going rate," and emptied his wallet. He asked for an appointment for the following week. "If you have any friends like you, I love to get tag teamed," he added. Nick nodded and smiled as he left. He returned home with a stack of twenties and a business plan.

April 15th. After saying yes to the hairy antiques dealer, I'm making more money than I did at my old job, in cash! I didn't think I'd be that good at it, but I've been told by more than one guy that I'm a natural, whatever that means? I think my background in the service industry helps. I'm punctual and professional. Last week, one guy answered the door, looked at his watch, and said, "Oh! You're actually here!" I guess other guys keep him waiting.

Nick hadn't been at his last job for very long before the bust, so he had the least amount of seniority when the layoffs started. "First in, first out," the human resources manager said with a pouty grimace as she handed him a box. The freelance work, scant as it was, made a good cover story for his new career. He had a sole confidante he could talk to about hustling. His friend Dean had been a party promoter who'd turned to sex work after New York nightlife was shut down by the Giuliani administration. "I used to throw parties," he'd say, and after a beat: "Now I *am* the party."

Nick had been keeping his diary in a fairly pretentious leather-bound journal with hot pressed pages and gilded edges he'd gotten as a Christmas present from his mom. He began writing a little recap of every call, with details like address, rate, and preferences. On late night phone calls, he would read entries to Dean, who would laugh and laugh, identifying with the

absurd scenarios he'd documented, while delighting in Nick's earnest approach to the work.

May 12th. These younger boys won't travel to Jersey but I don't mind. He was a tickle fetishist who booked a room at the Holiday Inn. He wore a wedding band. It was a pretty tame scene. I restrained his hands over his head and tickled his underarms, and also threatened to tickle him harder if he didn't open his mouth. Then he flipped the script on me, holding me down and tickling my feet, legs, ass, and underarms. I was fine with it until the tickle toys came out. I could even deal with the 1" sable paintbrush, but when he brought out an electric toothbrush, I was done. Still, I like being a *service provider to the whole tri-state area. Sometimes I feel like one of the late-shift utilities workers I saw on the bus ride back from Fort Lee. $300.*

Nick met up with Dean at the Cock, the bar where Dean used to throw his notoriously frisky party featuring naked go-go dancers. The police had raided the party repeatedly, and the health department issued code violations until he was forced to shut it down.

"I've noticed a decline in my weekly sales. I'm down something like twenty percent," complained Nick. He still had some regulars, like the hairy antiques dealer, and Headmaster, the guy he'd surprised by being on time. "It's still pretty good money, but the hours…" he continued.

Dean sucked on his straw and cruised a guy hovering by the door.

"I've been keeping to a savings plan, basically peeling a twenty off the top and stuffing it in a shoebox under the bed," to which Dean registered amazement.

"Wow, all my income goes to expenses…"

"I'm guessing that the word 'expenses' is doing a lot of work in your answer," Nick replied.

Dean laughed his thunderous laugh, then continued: "You were riding the newcomer bump. Now comes the slump. When you're fresh meat everyone wants you. We've all been there…" He'd become something of a mentor to Nick. He'd familiarized him with all these kinks and fetishes Nick had only read about. "You could say Dean showed me the ropes," Nick once joked to a bondage enthusiast as he worked through his bowlines.

June 5th. Dean called me in for a double with one his regulars, an older, well-preserved gay guy who lives down by Wall Street, a Lycra fetishist. He had a collection of underwear, singlets, jocks and Speedos. As we tried the items on he got more excited. *We wound up in used jocks, smoking ciga-rettes, playing into this fantasy of a couple of horny bros hanging out after a game. He loved being designated to service us. On the way out I noticed yesterday's crossword puzzle on the kitchen table. I said, "Oh! I do the cross-words, too," and gave him the answer to 32-across. This seemed to annoy him, and he all but pushed us out the door. Dean yelled at me for ruining the fantasy. $200.*

Dean's call interrupted Nick's afternoon sleep.

"Hey, I've got one I can't do. A raunch daddy. West Village. Two-fifty."

"A *what?*"

"Benito's a super guy. He's actually kind of a famous Mexican nov-elist. He likes guys ripe and sweaty. No deodorant, no cologne. He'll sniff your pits and your crotch and even your sweaty ass."

Nick hesitated, but Dean kept pitching.

"I think he'd really like you. He digs more natural guys." Dean en-hanced his physique with steroids (from Mexico, as a matter of fact). "It takes time to work up a stink, and I'm just too busy."

Nick took Benito's number, and after getting home from another grind of a session with the hairy antiques dealer, called him. They had a polite conversation and scheduled an appointment for the follow-ing day. The hairy antiques dealer was Nick's most reliable regular; he saw him at least once a week. Nick was happy to have a regular but grew weary of his demands. He wanted a full-on boyfriend experience, which Nick felt unsuited to provide, especially in light of his last rela-tionship review. Headmaster once called him a "Latin stud for hire," and Nick felt that was an apt description of the experience he offered. *I can be that guy, at least for an hour,* he thought.

On the morning of his appointment with Benito, Nick ran laps around the park and then headed over to the workout area for some pull-ups. It was crowded with neighborhood chulos, packing large in their baggy sweatpants and giving Nick slight nods. He skipped putting on deodorant, and came to enjoy tracking the developing odor wafting out of his warm pockets as he ran errands. Benito seemed to believe that he'd be getting two or three days of funk, so Nick fretted that today's sweat in yesterday's socks and underwear wouldn't be enough. He decided to bike across town for added effect.

"Please come in," Benito said at the door, and he leaned in to get a whiff as Nick crossed his threshold. With a delicate touch, he placed a turquoise envelope on the dresser. "Hello, I'm Nick," he said, and shook his hand. Benito pulled him into an embrace, inhaling deeply of his ripe body. He raised his head, closed his eyes, and his mouth formed an aficionado's smile which was somehow perfectly horizontal.

"Nick…Dean said I'd like you and I do."

He undressed as Benito shed his robe. The air thickened with Nick's funk, and the two strangers were bathed in this potent broth. Benito's fat tongue found Nick's mouth. He wedged his nose in Nick's armpit, inhaling and licking; Nick raised his arm, giving him full access. He licked the salt off of Nick's torso; Nick impulsively tasted it, too. When Benito lowered himself, Nick was impressed with the sight of this dignified man worshipping at his ripe feet. "Your body is a feast," Benito muttered as he peeled off his socks.

Nick pocketed the envelope without even counting the money; by now he could tell by the thickness. Though they hadn't discussed it, he was sure he'd be seeing Benito again.

Nick was surprised to hear back from the Lycra fetishist. He supposed he'd gotten over the crossword puzzle slight. Since his call with

Benito, he was aware of all the synthetic odors he encountered in his daily routine. The soap in the shower smelled like rest stop air freshener. The shampoo was fruity, for some reason. The lotion gave a hint of coconut, which on its own wasn't bad, but didn't combine well with the rest stop air freshener smell or the fruity hair smell. His clothes had a false-freshness detergent smell, which was distinct from the stale-sweat-trapped-in-synthetic-fibers smell coming off the Lycra fetishist's sports gear collection. He paid Nick the same rate as the first time when it was a double with Dean, which was a little short for a solo.

Benito returned to New York and called Nick for another session. He split his time between New York City and Mexico City, where he had a family. He was a visiting professor in Comparative Literature. In trying to understand Benito, Nick read an article about scent as the source of attraction and how pheromones are powerful sexual signals. Newly woke, he seethed against the systemic repression of human nature represented by the regime of personal care products.

June 21st. I enjoy giving Benito his immaterial pleasure, and stiffening my lean body against his soft folds. To all the other guys, I'm a fuck puppet. Benito takes his pleasure on another level. It's not just another fetish. I think of most fetishes—like the Lycra guy or the tickler—as substituting things for emotions. Benito is on some other trip. He has unlocked my sense of smell, which I guess I have neglected. I spent the afternoon shopping for unscented soap and detergent. $260.

On Benito's next stay in New York, he brought Nick a copy of his novel and some *alfajores* from a cake shop in Mexico City. Nick had made the switch to unscented products at home and only wore deodorant when it was really called for. He expected to get complaints, but instead men and women were drawn to him in public settings in what seemed like supernatural patterns. "I guess nature *is* super," Nick announced to one particular swarm in Tompkins Square Park.

After repeat sessions whenever Benito was in town, Nick moved into his apartment. He'd done a fair number of in-calls in his sublet—the landlord had questioned all the traffic—and it didn't really feel like home anymore, if it ever did. Benito's place, with its clean lines and soft tones, was sheltering and placid, like a hotel in a foreign capital. It had well-designed built-ins and the lights were on dimmers, and Benito had cleared a closet and a nightstand for him. He also left detailed instructions on the care of his plants. There was a giant aloe with spiky spears in the window by the kitchen. *He is a desert dweller you must not drown him,* he wrote.

July 31st. I saw the hairy antiques dealer again, who told me he was spending next month with his lover in New Hope. He invited me to visit, offering to put me up in a nearby hotel. Honestly I was relieved. He can be so clingy. Of course, he was extra clingy knowing that he probably wouldn't see me again for a while. I found myself thinking about Benito while faking my way through the session. There's no one else like him. He doesn't go for any false projections of romance. $220.

Nick would only go on calls when Benito was out of town; sometimes he would even tell him about them. Though Benito wasn't jealous, Nick liked maintaining this boundary. He'd clean the apartment naked, working up a funk so that he'd be ready for his return. He lay around reading Benito's novel in the original Spanish. "Translation is impossible, I'm afraid," Benito once said of the matter. With his vestigial Spanish reading skills, it would take him a long time to get through a chapter, but he had time. He'd make lists of words he didn't understand.

Shortly after moving into Benito's, Nick met up with Dean back at the Cock. Dean had just finished a call with a black john with Antebellum fantasies. Dean sincerely enjoyed the psychodrama of race play, but it made Nick uncomfortable.

"I think I'm in love with Benito," Nick confessed over a beer.

"Who's Benito?" asked Dean.

"You set me up with him. The Mexican writer in the West Village?"

"Oh, raunch daddy," Dean said with laughter. "You can't go falling in love with your johns. You'll go out of business!"

"Not all of them, just Benito," Nick replied.

"You're looking for love in all the wrong places," he scolded his friend with country music lyrics. "And by the way, you stink."

Is there such a thing? Nick wondered as he sniffed his pits.

In anticipation of Benito's return, Nick had prepared a list of words and phrases from his novel he couldn't find in the Spanish-English dictionary. They were mostly Mexican slang terms, along with some place names; the list would provoke a long conversation about the characters in the novel, interlaced with details of Benito's own life in Mexico City.

Nick was sprawled naked on the sofa writing in his diary when Benito walked in carrying bags of groceries, having promised Nick a lavish feast.

"I prepare for you *caña de filete con puré.*" said Benito.

"What's that?"

"Don't worry, *gringuito.* It's steak and potatoes." They laughed. "What are you reading? That is not my novel..." Benito asked with mock indignation.

"I'm writing, not reading. It's my diary."

"Hmm, another writer in the family. May I?" asked Benito, sliding alongside him to read: *I've been hustling all this year and it's mostly bearable. I try to keep the regulars interested and meet my weekly sales goals. I pride myself on being on time and delivering the goods. I'm never without my kit: condoms, lube, mints, lip balm, spare jockstrap, moist towelettes, eye drops, zinc lozenges, pain pills, an emergency twenty. What I didn't count on was the intimacy. It has changed me. I've found something to love about every single john.*

Benito picked his head up and paused to consider. "I enjoy your phrases. They remind me of your arched feet." He bent to kiss them and inhale their complicated notes. "Planted on the ground assertively, yet arched over the horizon, like mangrove roots. Like them, briny, and pulsing with vigor. *Puta madre*, I can be so fucking florid."

"I've learned a lot from hustling," Nick said.

"Oh? For example?"

"About desire. Not everyone can express what they want, like you can. Or even know. It's all coded. Sometimes I have to figure it out before I can deliver."

"You've persuaded me. You're a mechanic of longings, *gringuito*."

"Also how to glide past reception at elegant hotels…"

"A very useful skill…"

The feast was impeccable. Benito flamed the beef with Mezcal, the way he'd had it in one of his favorite restaurants back home. After the feast, Nick gave himself to Benito with an abandon he hadn't ever accessed before. He merged with Benito—his lover, his john, his professor, his aficionado—as they revered his body together. They razed all the boundaries between them: age, language, culture, power, money, the Rio Grande, the dry plains of the Southwest. Sprawled in bed, the novelist at his feet, he gloated over his ex-boyfriend's bad review: *I'll show you emotional availability!* Though the thought that he'd been brought to this place of emotional availability while hustling pricked at the afterglow.

Some days later, Nick returned to the apartment to find his diary perched on the dresser where Benito left his turquoise envelopes. Beneath the diary were twelve such envelopes, and on the last page was a note written in red.

Nueva York, 16 de Septiembre del 2004

Querido, *it's Benito. Of course you know from my pedantic handwriting. I beg forgiveness for sticking my nose* (jaja) *in your diary. I haven't told you something about your bounty of pleasures. Your body somehow brings back remembrances of the lost idyll of my youth. Your musky ass an overripe* melón chino *snapped off the vine, dew glistening on its skin, cracked open on the* metate. *Your underarms the neighbors' brick chimneys, commingling and thickening flavors of fruit and legume and pepita on their hearths, an alchemy of passion and earth. The touch of your pampered fingers that of my tutor, a boy just a few years older than me, who was later murdered by* Los Halcones. *Of course, your cum is my own* tepache de piña. *How I long for our unholy acts from my patio in* Coyoacán. *All is illusion except for your odor,* gringuito. *Let me also remind you that it is quite inconvenient—given my populist and anti-imperialist leanings—to be so enraptured by your capitalist body. You dominate me completely without raising a hand yet here I am colonizing your pages. Sometimes when I grade my students' compositions I hide lurid suggestions in the commentary.*

I will not return. The university has declined to renew my appointment. I suspect they have capitulated to pressure coming out of the El Encino *melodrama. It's a small price to pay for defending our democracy, such as it is. Please stay in the apartment and maintain the* plantitas. *Beny.*

Nick lowered his nose to the page and inhaled, detecting hints of tobacco and vetiver from Benito's absent fingers. His tears plonked on his lover's words, tracking through the red ink and pooling along the page's gilded edge.

THREE-WAY CALLS

Vinny Dazzle met Red at the Cock some time after Giuliani had launched his salvo against porno theaters and night clubs. The then-Mayor of New York City displayed a petty vindictiveness when it came to other New Yorkers having fun, this during the period he was fucking his mistress in the Emergency Command Center he'd built—against all rational advice—in the World Trade Center. Red Hansen was himself a New York landmark, like a skyscraper or a tourist attraction. He towered over most humans at nearly seven feet tall, his pale, sculpted face topped with a shock of red hair, and had been a famous, or infamous, nightlife impresario for nearly two decades.

It was Red Hansen who'd gotten his start taking over his neighborhood bodega for a series of outlaw after-hours parties. He'd stow the bodega's cats in his apartment. Nearly naked bartenders served beer out of the refrigerator cases while the Syrian owner's bi-curious son made sandwiches for the revelers. It was Red Hansen who had sledgehammered a brick wall in the back of Club Galaxy and took over the adjacent abandoned theater for his famous Tuesday night party. Rock stars, heiresses, and dope fiends alike would crawl through the rubble to dance in the orchestra pit. These were some of Red's past glories, but with Giuliani's assault on nightlife in full swing, he'd lost most of his gigs. The night he and Vinny met, he was off-duty, cruising in the bar's notoriously frisky back room, a surviving affront to the Mayor's moralist crusade.

Vinny was a stacked Italian stud with a heavy brow and a bright smile made brighter still by a gold filling in an upper bicuspid. He'd grown up on the Lower East Side and had worked in some of the same bars and clubs Red had worked in, first as a bartender, later as a go-go dancer—until the crowds got too grabby—and most recently as a bouncer. They had somehow never run into each other before. Vinny hadn't planned on fucking around in the back room that night because he was wearing a thick gold chain he'd just bought himself, but was drawn in by Red's deep laughter.

Red and Vinny sized each other up like competing alphas of a troop, sniffing, grunting, throwing looks through the dark. Eyes in the room shifted towards them as they postured dominance at each other in turns. Their sexual encounter was more performative than passionate; Red was ever the exhibitionist, while Vinny summoned some old go-go moves. As they drew more and more attention, someone pushed aside the black curtain from the room's single window. Their large bodies glowed with sweat in the incidental light, and after Red's thunderous climax and Vinny's fountain-like display, witnesses filed out of the room in awe, snapping, fanning themselves, gasping. Red proposed they go to Odessa for a late-night meal, and on the way out, turned to Vinny and said, "I have a feeling we will make better friends than lovers," to which Vinny shrugged.

Over burgers, they realized they were both soon tuning 40, and within a few days of each other. "Another gemini. I was right, we couldn't possibly be lovers," said Red, who invested far more meaning in astrology than Vinny. Red then launched into a comical retelling of his upbringing in—and escape from—his WASPy Connecticut family, who expressed little and drank much. In short order, the two became friends.

Red would take Vinny as his plus one for various openings, fashion shows, and parties to which he'd been invited. Vinny got Red a bouncer gig at Scores, a straight strip club on the West Side. Red was taller than all the other bouncers, but much skinnier, so Vinny put him in a boxy black suit. He looked the part, but would fag out when the girls showed up for their shifts, and was generally way too chatty to maintain the deadpan demeanor the work required.

As the mayoral crusade shut down his parties one by one, as he lost the Scores gig, a nearly broke Red embarked on a new career as an escort. He advertised on rentboy.com as 'Big Red' with a suite of photos one of his fashion photographer friends had shot of him against a velvet background. As the new cock on the block, Red experienced a surge in popularity. Vinny was intrigued.

"How's the escorting thing working out for you?" Vinny asked one night as they were on their way to an art gallery.

"It's great, I'm a natural, or that's what they say. More than one guy has told me that I smell like raw meat, but they love it," Red replied, laughing thunderously.

"Oh yeah?"

"It's just like club promoting, only *I'm* the party," he said in triumph.

Red found that he attracted various types of clients: submissives, size queens, devoted cocksuckers, foot fetishists, advanced fisting bottoms, giant chasers, tight-assed 'sons' looking to be violated by 'dad'. He was especially drawn to such role-play scenarios, and soon a whole universe of interpersonal dramas opened up to him, to which he happily applied his theatrical training. He had a devoted regular who was a television actor with a role in a long-running police drama. He'd outfitted Red's studio apartment with a bamboo cage for protracted Viet Cong prisoner-of-war scenarios. Red was repeatedly cast as a Viking pillager for historical rape fantasies. Vinny had narrowed his eyes straining to understand when Red told him about the calls he'd taken from married men who were into cuckolding. For these clients, Red would be enlisted to fuck their wives, while the wives demeaned their husbands. "They all seem to live in the Jersey suburbs," Red observed. Closer to home, sometimes Red would get to the door and the client would recognize him and cry, "Oh my god, you're Red Hansen!" and slam the door shut; but there were those who recognized him and turned out to be huge fans, opening their hearts, their wallets, and their legs for Big Red.

Red proposed bringing Vinny in on what he called a "three-way call." In this role Red was part hustler, casting agent, and pimp. Their first call together was in a midtown hotel, an out-of-towner who wanted to be beaten, "with no limits," by a pair of robbers. Red and Vinny wore sunglasses and ball caps and stomped through the lobby, while Red coached Vinny. "Just fuck him up however you want, there's no safe word," he instructed. Vinny nodded. Red retrieved a key card from the reception desk and the two made their way to the guy's floor. They entered and swept the room, finding the agreed-upon sum on the nightstand. Their client was cowering in the bathroom. Vinny dragged the unassuming, middle-aged man by his hair and threw him onto the bed, then proceeded to hit him with calculated punches. Red grabbed Vinny and whispered, "Let me in, we need to work him together." Vinny had disassociated while planning where the blows would land, the gut, the chin, the shoulder. He snapped back to the present and watched as Red energetically wailed away. The poor out-of-towner broke out of character and begged them to leave as he collected his dental bridge from off the floor. Red shrugged and walked out, a puzzled Vinny lagging behind him.

"Red? Should we help him?" asked Vinny, as he tried to catch up.

"He said no limits," answered Red. "People don't even know what they want."

In the elevator, Red counted off $300 in twenties and handed it to Vinny, saying, "You had the spirit, but next time, work with me a little. We're scene partners."

"Gotcha," Vinny replied, counting the bills. It was more than he made on a full shift at Scores.

Vinny was over at his mom's apartment on Rivington Street eating lasagna when his phone rang. The call came from Red's number, but a frail voice asked for him.

"Is this Vinny?"

"Yea, who's this?" He crawled out onto the fire escape for some privacy.

"I'm one of Red's regulars. He's passed out here, I'm not sure what to do…"

"Is he okay?"

"I believe so, but the situation, as you can imagine, is a bit awkward."

Vinny got the man's address and jumped in a cab to the West Village. Red had opened his eyes by the time he arrived, but was groggy and disoriented. The owlish priss of a man who'd called Vinny hovered unhelpfully. Vinny asked him what Red had taken, and the man showed him several prescription bottles, oxycontin in various doses. "I have a chronic pain condition," the man said defensively, pulling the bottles back. "I think Red may have been naughty and taken one from the medicine cabinet." Vinny returned to Red's side. While the man was stashing his bottles away, Vinny gave him a bump of speed, which had the desired effect. Red roused enough to get downstairs and into a cab back to Vinny's place.

"Take this for the taxi," said the man, pushing some bills on Vinny as he walked Red to the door. Vinny noticed crustiness around his lips before he lurched away.

"Thanks," answered Vinny, "and don't worry."

Once he got Red home, Vinny checked his pupils, and had him splash water on his face. He tested his speech for coherence. Red looked around to assess his surroundings. Having never been in Vinny's apartment before, he was impressed with its modern design and orderliness. His own cramped studio, usually a mess, was furnished with mismatched street finds, and much of the space was lately taken up by that bamboo cage.

"Your place is gorgeous," said Red, fingering a hand-thrown ceramic bowl.

"Thanks," said Vinny, inflating with pride.

"Have you considered doing in-calls?"

"Now I know you're back to your senses." Red laughed. "No way, this is my sanctuary."

Vinny made Red a smoothie, got him settled onto the sofa, and dug out a blanket that would cover his tall frame. Red watched cartoons until he fell asleep, and when Vinny sensed that the danger had fully passed, he went into his bedroom and collapsed.

In the morning, Red was gone before Vinny awoke, having left him a note in the bowl that read, 'Off to rehearsal, IOU!' Red was scheduled to perform in a sketch at Wigstock that summer.

◆

It had been some weeks and Vinny hadn't seen or heard from Red since his near-overdose. They hadn't worked a three-way together for even longer. Vinny assumed that Red was busy with rehearsals; in truth, Red had a new client, a Scarsdale dentist with a pied-à-terre on the Upper East Side. Red had gotten himself emotionally entangled with both the dentist and his wife, who'd caught her husband with Red in the apartment on an unannounced visit. The dentist was wearing a leather harness, and Red was flogging him with a cat-o-nine-tails. These items had been newly purchased by the dentist, the packaging left on the kitchen table. Her discovery prompted a dramatic scene with screaming and sobbing from both spouses. Red sought to console the dentist's wife, who somehow arrived at the notion that she deserved sex from Red, too. Red came to see her point, plus the dentist was paying. Her overdone cries of pleasure as they fucked seemed meant for her husband, who was waiting in the living room. The three-sided relationship devolved into a co-dependent, romantic-obsessive love triangle. Once it flamed out for good, Red reached out to Vinny.

In addition to the various categories of admirers, Red also received a fair number of calls from Black guys. Some of them simply had a predilection for white meat, and meat didn't get any whiter than Red's, its pale sheath nearly translucent, a bluish vein pulsing just below its tautness. Some of them requested race play, a form of domination in which taboo, racist terms are employed as an aspect of humiliation. Red enjoyed these calls immensely, finding them as cathartic as his Black clients. He was switchable for these scenarios, meaning he was willing to dole out racial abuse as well as submit to it.

Red had a semi-regular named Jay, a media executive who lived in a well-appointed prewar apartment in Murray Hill. Jay hired Red to enact his antebellum fantasies. He'd requested a second white guy, prompting Red's call to Vinny.

"I have a regular, he wants a three-way for the next session, it's

$250."

"I'm in," answered Vinny. He was saving to buy his mom a flat-screen television.

"His name is Jay, he's a cool guy. I play the plantation owner, he's my slave, and I punish him for his disobedience."

"Wait, is he Black?"

"Of course, it wouldn't make much sense if he weren't," Red answered.

"Hmm, I dunno..." Vinny said.

Red seemed not to hear him. "You're going to play my cousin from a neighboring plantation. You've come for a visit and we head back behind the barn, so you can watch how Masser Red doles out punishment to his insolent slave," he explained.

"But..."

"You'll be fine. I'll give you lines. Just answer me with things like, 'No doubt he deserves it, cousin,' or, 'He's your property, cousin.'"

"Do I have to do a Southern accent?"

"It'll help."

On the appointed night, the two arrived at Jay's apartment. Jay, who had hooded eyes, short, tight curls, and a trim beard, was about the same age as his hires. He appeared at the door in denim overalls, already sweating, mopping his brow with a cloth, and fully submissive to Red. Red launched into his Southern accent and ordered him to the "back of the barn," which was actually a hallway leading to the terrace. There Red rattled off a litany of complaints about his slave—laziness, insolence, taking inappropriate liberties with a certain newly-arrived young slave—peppered with choice racial slurs. Vinny had let out a nervous laugh when Red first launched into his tirade, which prompted stern looks from both Red and Jay, and threatened to derail the scene.

Jay was bowed in deference, and muttered, "Yes, Masser Red," over and over.

Red then turned to Vinny, who had watched this scene in silent unease after they'd reproached him, wincing every time Red used a slur. He said, "Now you'll see how I keep these d____ in line, cousin," to which Vinny answered a mumbled, "He deserves it, cousin." Red flashed a disapproving look at Vinny, then turned to Jay, and barked, "down on your knees, boy."

He instructed Vinny to tighten his thighs around Jay's head so as to hold him in position while he whipped his back with a switch that Jay kept hanging on the wall.

Red then ordered Jay to service him and his cousin in turns. This part of the scene was more conventional and less disagreeable to Vinny, who responded with conviction, and even a touch of a Southern lilt, when Red complimented his slave's skills. The scene concluded with Jay on his knees savoring his degradation before a standing Red and Vinny, drenched in sweat, his face and neck spotted with their milky ejaculations.

Jay wiped his head with his cloth and came to his feet. The spell was broken. His natural speaking voice emerged as he thanked each of his hires, shaking their hands, slipping them each an envelope. He returned the switch to where it hung on the wall, like a significant artifact, and walked his hires to the door. He was affable, making some light conversation about New York living. Vinny got the message that there was to be no processing of what had just taken place. Red made a show of cheer, clapping Jay on the back and saying, "See you next time," although it also came out as a half question. Jay answered, "Of course," as he shut the door.

Red hailed a cab back downtown, and once on their way, he and

Vinny opened their envelopes, counted their money, and high-fived.

"He seems like a nice guy," said Vinny.

"Oh, he's great," answered Red, "but you have to be more committed to the scene. You nearly snapped him out of it."

"Sorry, I'll keep it together next time," answered Vinny.

Red shrugged, and the cab pulled up in front of Vinny's place.

◆

Once again, weeks went by without Vinny hearing from Red. Wigstock was approaching, and he thought he'd at least get invited to hang out backstage. Maybe Red was mad at him because of his lack of commitment to the role of the slaveholder's cousin from a neighboring plantation? When a call finally came in from a Connecticut number, he was relieved, until he heard a woman's voice.

"Is this Vinny?"

"Yes, who's speaking?"

Vinny, this is Janice, Red's mom. I'm afraid I have some bad news."

"Oh…"

"We've lost him, dear. A New York City policeman notified me, they think it was an ooh-ver-dose of painkillers," she said, drawing out the word with some exasperation, as if it were a nuisance to even say. Vinny heard Janice take a drink, then she recounted what she'd learned of Red's final night. "He was in an apartment in the West Village," she said. Vinny winced at the recollection of that prissy trick. She wondered, did Vinny know anything about the man who lived there? Vinny stammered, unsure of what to reveal, but agreed to meet with her in person. She explained she'd be coming into the city that Saturday. There would be something of a memorial service at the bodega where

Red had thrown those notorious parties years ago. The former owner's son, who'd made sandwiches back then, had taken over the place, and had arranged for a gathering of Red's neighbors and nightlife friends.

The evening of the memorial service, Vinny put on his best black suit and made his way to the bodega. It was already full, the crowd overflowing out the doors and onto the sidewalk. It was sweltering hot, and the bodega owner graciously made the rounds, inside and out, offering cold drinks. Vinny recognized Janice Hansen immediately; she was a very tall, elegant woman with auburn hair, in a smart black dress and a little hat with a veil. Vinny introduced himself and Janice peeled them away from the crowd, taking him by the arm for a walk around the block.

"Thank you for coming," Janice said.

"Of course, Red was my friend," answered Vinny.

"What about these painkillers? Was he an addict?"

"I don't know, I had some idea, but didn't realize it was so serious." He didn't want to reveal too much to Red's mother. "He was good at keeping up appearances…"

"They've confirmed it was an ooh-ver-dose, but won't confirm accidental or intentional."

"One thing I can say for sure, Red did not want to die," said Vinny.

She shuddered, then found her voice. "Thank you Vinny, I believe you." She steered him back to the bodega, where the crowd had grown larger. One by one, Red's friends stood up on an improvised stage–a wooden box with an old rug thrown over it–and told stories of Red's good-natured antics. The sweaty crowd expressed emotions in waves– anger, sadness, hilarity, and fond remembrance–fanning themselves and drinking. Janice held on tightly to Vinny's arm, occasionally drinking gin from a flask. Red's father was nowhere to be seen; Vinny thought it better not to ask.

The New York Times sent a reporter from their Styles section, who quoted an attendee saying that Red's death represented "the final nail in the coffin of New York nightlife." There were hustlers, strippers, neck-craning socialites, fashionistas, and drag queens in attendance, along with Red's downstairs neighbor, an ancient Ukrainian woman in a housedress. Many of Red's tricks appeared, though not the man he and Vinny had beaten, nor the man in whose apartment Red had overdosed. The television actor was there in dark sunglasses, along with one of the Jersey cuckolds. The Scarsdale dentist and his wife arrived by limo, bearing babka.

Jay appeared, in an impeccable black suit, and hugged Janice like family, while her face registered resignation. "I can't look at the things I see, for they are just temporary," Jay half-sang, releasing her. "Red was very special. He was special to me..." He cried profusely, mopping his tears away with a purple silk handkerchief. Janice's disdain for this stranger's show of emotion filtered through her frozen politesse.

"Thank you so much for coming," she said blandly. She eyed Vinny, who emerged from his confusion over the scene to rescue her.

"Jay," he said, extending his hand. Janice lunged to greet another guest.

"Oh, yea, you're Red's cousin, ah, friend..." Jay said, shaking his hand.

"Vinny," he said. Jay nodded. "Right, Vinny," he answered. Was it possible that Vinny heard a note of disdain when Jay said his name?

"I understand if this is awkward," Vinny offered.

"Awkward? My heart is broken, you know? Red was the deal. He understood me like no one else."

"I know what you mean..."

"I don't think you do," Jay answered, restored to outer calmness. "Everybody love Red's meat, his raw meat attraction…Red got me in here," he said, thumping his chest, then Vinny's. Vinny's face flushed above the knot of his tie. "What I need, it is what it is, with all of this…" he said, gesturing at the scene before him. "I'm not wrong, it's all right. And I pay for it, you know? All you had to do was work it out."

Vinny froze in place, stung. The bodega, scene of this messy out-pouring of emotions for Red, was just a couple of blocks from where he'd grown up, where, despite his notable smile, he'd lived his life of pulled punches, of deadpan demeanor, of lack of commitment to the role. Another speaker took the platform.

"I'm sorry, it was just uncomfortable…" Vinny said.

"Oh right, because it's all about your comfort…" Jay said with a sardonic smile, and moved on to shake the dentist's hand.

PART III:
AFTERLIVES

RITA DOLORES

On a December night outside of a midtown New York City strip club, Rita Dolores cocked an eyebrow at young Max Maynard, glanced down at the velvet rope, then lowered her pointed finger as if it was a blade slicing through meat. Max had been shuffling forward on the line while trying not to gawk at the club kid's outrageous get-ups, not liking his own chances of getting in. He'd noticed Rita whispering to one of her doormen as he advanced into her view. The club kids stopped their excitable chatter to witness as the doorman unclasped the rope and nodded him through.

As Max passed between the stanchions he extended his hand to Rita. She strained to elongate her fingers while rotating her wrist, willing her rough hand to appear delicate. She then placed her hand atop his, as if he were about to escort her into a ballroom.

"Aren't you a tall drink of water," she said with theatrical, accented diction, then she drew close to his ear and mouthed an indecent sipping sound. Too embarrassed to reply, Max smiled awkwardly and entered the club.

Rita's sharp allure on that night in 1986 would come back to Max decades later, opening more than a door.

◆

It was Max's college roommate, Nico, who'd told him about the party. As the only two so-called minorities in their incoming class, Nico and Max had been paired by their school's housing office and were unlikely friends. Nico was an art major, a scion of Argentine industrialists, an out, flamboyant party boy, while Max, son of public school teachers from the African-American enclave of Rosedale, was a sexually confused English major prone to moody self-absorption. Nico saw some potential in Max and took him on as a project. "I might just turn him out, or at least polish off some of that outer borough provincialism," he'd once said of the project. Nico was running a fever the night of the party. His first semester of sophomore year having ended, Max took an uncharacteristically bold plunge and decided to go alone. Nico lent him an oversized jacket by a Japanese designer, which he wore with white high-tops, black jeans, and an old Specials t-shirt. Before he hit the street, Nico spiked out his twists in a wild mess inspired by Basquiat.

Rita was the hostess of the party. During the week, Bentley's was a strip club that catered to working men. The strippers were kept busy weekday nights with the after-work scene, but didn't attract crowds on weekends, so the management gave Saturday night over to Rita for what they called queer night. Rita had a stately bearing which contrasted with her filthy banter. Her fans loved her salacious humor as much as they were fascinated by her illusion. Though she was on the taller side, and delicate only in certain features, she was beautiful. She had a thin neck and favored jeweled chokers. Her cheekbones were carved, her nose straight, and her earlobes dainty. Her complexion was smooth and tan, her makeup heavy, in the style of women her age. An older queen on line had assessed her look: "She's giving dusky Kat Hepburn tonight," which his friend affirmed with a triple snap.

In the ranking system of drag queens, Rita was unclockable; she could pass as a woman out on the street. "Even in daylight she serve," another of her fans standing behind Max had said as they waited on line, perhaps an exaggeration. Max had overheard gossip that she lived on Long Island and would take the train in full drags. Little was truly known about her private life, although there were rumors that she was married with a wife and children. Unlikely as they seemed, these rumors lent her an inscrutable air.

One of Bentley's regular strippers, Lady Hennessy, had cajoled Rita into booking her for the opening party. Her act included a variation on the standard magic trick of pulling an endless series of multi-colored handkerchiefs out of a hat, a bag, or the magician's mouth. Lady Hennessey pulled the handkerchiefs out of her pussy, to the scandalized delight of the opening night crowd. She rounded out the assortment of lip-syncing drag queens, go-go dancers, and burlesque performers Rita had assembled, and the party became the hot ticket. Rita closed the night herself with a lip sync performance of "El Carbonero," a lament for the working man delivered with tempestuous zeal.

His visit to the club on opening night would not be Max's last. Nico was feeling better when the next of Rita's parties was announced. "I'm not missing out again. You're coming with me," Nico said as he threw another outfit together for Max. The line was even longer than that first night, the crowd more agitated; only Rita's stern door presence kept it from frenzy. Rita craned her neck when she spotted Max on the line. "My tall drink of water," she said, while summoning her cocktail. The crowd parted, and Max introduced Nico to Rita, who shook his hand while angling her cheek towards Max for a kiss. Nico played it cool as they were whisked inside, but Max could tell he was impressed, even jealous.

Rita's selectiveness at the entry was backed up by two doormen, both enormous and unsmiling bodybuilders. One had reddish-brown skin, the other was pale and freckled, and they presented themselves with a certain symmetry: broad shoulders, broken noses, black suits with collarless jackets, vacant stares. It gave the impression that Rita held command over a vast realm. On his first visit, Max had stepped outside for some air and overheard them talking. One of them confessed it was his first time working on a gay night, while the other reassured him. "It's an easy gig, the queers don't fight," he said, to which his partner shrugged.

Once inside the club Nico commanded Max, "Go get us drinks, you're taller," and found his friends. The bar was operating efficiently until one of the bartenders cut himself on broken glass. A space cleared as Rita abandoned the door and barged through. She hiked up her sequined gown, leapt up onto the bar, swiveled, and dropped down into the service area. She started pulling draft beers two at a time with finesse. "It's on me, darlings, just don't get it *on* me," she said as she handed them off, brushing her gown between pours. "If I had a dollar for every time I said that…" she deadpanned, "and he didn't listen." She'd tamed and even charmed the impatient crowd by the time the bandaged bartender resumed his work.

Lady Hennessy was announced. Expecting a repeat of the act he'd seen, Max whispered to Nico: "Wait 'til you see this. She's *deeply* talented." Taking the stage wearing a raincoat, a sea captain's hat, and a studded bikini, she set the coat on the stage and performed a series of erotic contortions. Rising, she then opened her bikini top and cupped her ample breasts. After soaking in applause on their behalf, she squeezed and twisted them, spraying milk out onto the gasping crowd. Those up front were drenched in her abundant streams, making them duck for cover in horror, while delighting Max and Nico, safely out of range.

On their way out, the roommates saw Rita talking to Musto, the gossip columnist from the Village Voice. He'd given the party a glowing write-up, accounting for the bigger crowd. Musto was raving, "Gurl, that was a first. A lactation act…" They measured the impact of his article. "It's been a mixed blessing, let's put it this way…" Rita said witheringly, eyeing some out-of-towners. She caught sight of Max and flashed him a smile. Nico found a group of his friends at the door and sashayed over to them.

Max was looking back at Rita when a rangy man, wearing a beret, tinted glasses, and a brushy mustache, sidled up to him.

"Hey man, what's on tonight, can I set you up?" he asked.

"Oh, hey, uhh…." as Max stumbled to answer, Rita excused herself and hurried over.

"Leaving so soon?" she purred. She flashed the mustache a look.

"Yeah…class tomorrow…" answered Max.

Locking arms with him, she said, "Class. What subject? I could teach you."

"I'm sure you could…"

She got in close and whispered, "Steer clear of that one," then cackled loudly and said, in full voice, "Every man should experience the attentions of a true lady at least once…"

She walked Max back towards where she'd left Musto. They had a laugh over some club kid antics, and the mustache stalked away, eyeing another young man standing alone. Rita handed Max a matchbook from the hotel across the street, with '404' written on the inside cover in lipliner. He kissed her goodbye and was on his way.

Max never made it back to Rita's night at Bentley's. He moved on to other pursuits, while Nico eventually moved on to the next hot party.

Max never did take up Rita's offer for the attentions of a true lady. He's wasn't sure if it was real or if was to throw off the mustache. He'd been tempted to pay her a visit just to learn more about her. He kept the matchbook as a memento from his brief dalliance in nightlife.

◆

After graduating, Max took a job at the Village Voice. The pay was low and his regular beat was city politics. The corruption that threaded through the city left him too angry to cover the subject dispassionately. When the Long Island Daily offered him the crime beat, he jumped at it. Though it meant moving back in with his parents, he'd always wanted to be a breaking news reporter. Getting a call and rushing to the scene was what had attracted him to journalism in the first place.

After graduating, Nico rented a studio in DUMBO and painted large, colorful abstractions for corporate commissions. His canvasses sold for high dollars, and he spent the money the minute it was in hand, like he always did, on wild outfits and parties. He'd sneered when Max told him he was temporarily moving back to Rosedale: "You were always something of a momma's boy."

"Wherever you go, there you are," Max answered.

Max's beat had been quiet the day a tip came into the newsroom about a mummified body found stuffed in a trunk in a hotel storeroom. Among the scant details the source provided was the date the trunk had been left: December 1987. Max's boss had a hunch: the date tracked with a cold case, a missing person who'd lived in Mineola. Was the body in the trunk the missing Abel Jarvis? It was a long shot on a slow beat. His boss put Max on the case. Max took a train into the city, wondering if his boss was just putting him through his paces.

The Hotel Aberdeen: the name didn't register with Max until he saw the old marquee sign from down the block. His brief encounter with Rita Dolores flashed back at him, navigating the rapids of memory as a raft lashed together with contradictions: her rough hands, her penetrating gaze, her lewd fixation, her mothering care. He still had the matchbook she'd given him from this very hotel, pressed flat in a journal. Some lipliner had transferred onto the page, but the room number she'd written on the inside cover was still legible.

As Max hurried across the Garment District, the summer heat intensifying, a sweaty tough rolling a hand-truck stacked high with boxes gave him a sly nod. The hotel was covered in scaffolding, the coroner's truck parked out front. A splashy sign announced the building's planned redevelopment as a combined hotel and luxury condo. Max entered the lobby to find the crime scene cordoned off with yellow tape. Hotel guests ogled the young NYPD officer standing guard as they made their way to the elevator, as if he were a tourist attraction.

Max flashed his press credentials and the harried cop waved him down a corridor towards the storeroom. The coroner's team was processing the room. Through the open door he could see a large steamer trunk. It appeared to have been opened on a luggage stand, which had tipped over. The stand was askew, the suitcase broken open. The mummified body was a gruesome sight: the face wore a rictus of slow horrors, bones jutted through leathery skin, the whole artifact cast in a deep red-orange hue.

Just outside the door, Max noticed a small, squarish object steeped in the same red-orange color. He recognized it as a Hotel Aberdeen matchbook. It appeared that the impact of the suitcase hitting the floor had dislodged it, sending it skating across the terrazzo and through the doorway. That or it had been kicked into its present position, Max reasoned. Either way it was sloppy control of a crime scene. He felt strangely protective of the matchbook, knowing that he had one like it back home. His heart raced as he calculated his chances of picking it up without detection. The cop down the hall was busy brushing off some gawkers. He took a bandanna from his pocket then dropped his notebook. He swooped down and quickly collected the matchbook in the bandanna, hiding it behind the notebook. He was willing to risk interfering with the investigation, but didn't want to destroy evidence.

A guy on the Medical Examiner's team eyed him just as he stood up, blocking Max with his arms and giving him a hard stare. *He's pretty hot*, thought Max. Then Max spotted a woman he knew from the ME's office behind him. Even in her crime scene coverall, Ann Niebold was immediately recognizable to Max for her owlish appearance. It belied her thick Jersey accent and salty tongue. She'd hardly changed since Max had interviewed her about Michael Alig, the case of the club kid murderer. Back then, she'd confided in Max about the hazing she'd gotten as an out lesbian in the boy's club environment of the city's ME office. Max could see by her badge that she now was a Deputy. He was glad to see that she'd been promoted, and gladder still to have a contact on the case, but felt worse about tampering with evidence.

"Hello, Ann, it's been a while," Max shouted in her direction. She looked up from her work.

"Max!" she said, gesturing to her colleague to stand down. He shrugged, and resumed packing up. "I'd hug you, but I've got this shit on me...

"Completely understandable."

"What brings you to this mess?"

"I'm on the job, for the Long Island Daily. I see they made you

Deputy."

"First Deputy, thank you very much," she replied, brushing off her badge.

"Congrats. You paid your dues."

"Yea, I'm a god-damned trailblazer..." she rolled her eyes and looked back at the corpse.

"Not your first body in a trunk..."

"Don't fucking remind me." She bagged some of the red-orange powder. "This one appears to be packed in cinnabar, of all things. High concentrations of mercury, making it a containment scene to boot. Pretty ghoulish."

"Well, I'll let you get back to it. Come find me in the diner next door when you're done?"

"Sure thing. Give me fifteen."

The Aberdeen Diner was another holdout, a place that had served hot lunch plates to the area's workmen and secretaries for decades. It, too, would soon be replaced, to the dismay of its remaining regulars. Max grabbed a table up front and ordered some coffee. The matchbook seemed to be burning a hole in his pocket, but he'd have to wait to examine it. It was too risky to pull it out so close to the crime scene. After a tense wait, during which Max scribbled some notes, Ann made her way to the table.

"Thanks, just the ticket," she said, swigging at her cup.

"Of course. It's so good to see you again."

"I look the same, right? A little gray, but no worse for wear," she said, fussing with her hair. "But you! You just keep getting better looking. Are you till single?"

"Ha, still on that trip, trying to set me up?"

"Did you check out my assistant, Burke? The big guy by the door?

He was asking about you…You should call him, you can't tell with the coveralls, but that man has an ass on him…" she outlined his shapely posterior with her hands and wolf-whistled.

"Thanks, Ann, but I was really hoping you could help me with this case…"

"But why are you on it if you're at the Long Island paper?"

"The victim seems to match a missing person from '87. The man lived in Mineola."

"Ah, the plot thickens…I'll be your contact on the case, as long as you call Burke." She slid his card across the table. "Quid pro quo, Mr. Maynard."

Max took the card and nodded. "So what can you tell me about the cause of death?"

"At first glance? A blunt force trauma to the head presents, even with the body's condition. The blow was not that forceful, but could have triggered a TIA."

"A TIA?"

"An aneurysm. Not that common, but tell that to the unlucky bastard. For that, we'll have to wait for the autopsy. A bit of a challenge on mummified remains…"

"So that's your working theory?" Max asked.

"For now. I may find something else back at the lab," she answered.

"How could it have been overlooked all these years? Wouldn't there have been a smell?"

"It was stashed in an overflow space by the mechanical room. The whole area had a stench of death, probably rats…" She shuddered. "One of the guys on the demo crew brought it out to the storeroom and opened it, thinking he'd find lost treasure."

"Maybe whoever left it had a friend on the inside," Max speculated.

"Speaking of a friend on the inside…" Ann said with a licentious tone, "Are you gonna call Burke?" Max dutifully took out the card and dialed. Ann rubbed her hands together with glee.

After making a date with Burke, Max hugged Ann goodbye. He rushed over to Penn Station with the commuter herd. He found a seat on the train and pulled the matchbook out, handling it through the bandanna. The ink had faded, but it looked the same as his souvenir from Rita, with the sketch of the hotel and the phone number given in the old-fashioned exchange: PEnnsylvania 6-4500. The inside cover was printed with a jaunty 'Hello!' just like his, and below the print, he could make out the lipliner traces of room number 404.

◆

Linda Jarvis was weeding in her yard when Max pulled up to the house she'd lived in with Abel up until his disappearance.

"Mrs. Jarvis?"

"Who's asking?"

"Max Maynard from the Long Island Daily. It's about your late husband…"

"He's gone a long time. Why are you chasing ghosts?"

"A body was found this morning."

"No…" her walls crumbled. "Was that Abel? The body in the trunk?"

"The coroner just confirmed it from dental records."

"Why didn't they contact me?"

"I was told that the phone number they had for you was disconnected…"

"Oh…" she grasped the weeder in both hands. "Well, what happened to him?"

"They're investigating. All we know so far is that his body was packed in a trunk and stored in the old Hotel Aberdeen. It somehow went undetected all these years. They only found it now because they're renovating."

"Well, you might as well come in. I need a drink," she said, throwing down the weeder and turning towards the front door.

The Jarvis home was spotlessly clean and decorated in the mid-century style. Max peeked into the study, furnished with a teak desk set he coveted. The room was decorated with Nixon campaign memorabilia. Abel Jarvis had been a fan, and Mrs. Jarvis hadn't changed the décor.

"Mrs. Jarvis…"

"Linda. No one's called me that in years," she said, pouring whiskey into two tumblers.

"Linda. I know it's been a long time, but what can you tell me about your husband?"

"Abel was a cipher," she said, handing Max one of the tumblers, her hands trembling.

"You mean he didn't let you in?" he asked.

"Ha," she said, throwing back her shot. "He was a chemical salesmen, you know? He traveled most of the year. He kept his samples locked away in the garage. I knew his business trips weren't all business, let's put it that way. Once he called me to say he was in Hartford, but I found a matchbook in his jacket from a hotel in the city when he came back."

"The Aberdeen?"

"That's it, that's where they found him? There was something going on there…"

"Yes."

"Well, I'm glad they finally did. I haven't missed him all that much, if I'm being honest, but it's unsettling, the not knowing."

"I'm sure."

"His boss sent a crew to clear out the garage. The insurance company was suspicious, but eventually they paid out. Took 'em long enough."

"Oh?" Max took notes.

"I never told anyone about this, but a couple of weeks after he disappeared, I got an envelope with cash in the mailbox. No name, no note. I got another one a month later, then the insurance came through."

"Who do you think left it?"

She shrugged. "I assumed it was one of his business associates."

A patrol car pulled up to the house just as Linda was walking Max to the door. She rolled her eyes as Max made his way to his car and pondered his next move. He wondered about Rita Dolores. *Was she still alive?* Musto had covered her during her heyday in nightlife, but Max couldn't recall her given name ever being published. Who was the man behind Rita Dolores and how could he find him? Hoping for a lead, he changed direction and drove straight to the Aberdeen, just as the evening rush out of the city had started.

The investigators had wrapped up at the scene, and a demolition crew was waiting for word to get started on their overtime. Max made his way to the hotel's service entrance, in the rear of the building, and spotted a roll-off dumpster with some old wooden file cabinets. He checked the drawers and found several full of old-style registration cards. Just then, a compact stud on the work crew approached with a trash bin.

"Mind if I help myself to these, brother?" Max flashed his reporter's badge. "I'm doing a story on the hotel and might find something interesting."

"Knock yourself out," he replied.

Max grabbed two drawers full of cards out of the dumpster and hustled out of the service door before anyone could stop him.

After driving back to the office, Max spiked a coffee and poured over the cards. They dated from the mid-eighties, which tracked with what he was looking for, although the year had been occasionally left off. First he sorted the hundreds of names and addresses alphabetically by last name; then he thought to organize them by home address. Rita couldn't have been from too far off, he reasoned. Before he could finish sorting the guests by their home states, nearest to furthest, his eyes crossed and his head sunk onto the desk.

He awoke early the next morning with a stiff neck and a blinking realization. After organizing hundreds of cards first one way, then another, he realized he should be looking for recurring registrations under the same name, since Rita would have checked in every month for the years the party ran. After wading through common surnames, he set about looking for repeat registrants. In the New York pile, were about thirty cards filled out with stylish flourish by a Mr. Desiderio Terran of 215th Place in Bayside. He remembered the gossip about Rita riding the train in full drags. *Bayside has a Long Island Railroad stop,* he recalled.

While most sections of the cards were filled out by the registrant, the room numbers were in another hand. Scanning Mr. Terran's stack of cards, he'd been assigned the same room every time he checked in. It was room 404, just like on his matchbook, just like on the matchbook from the crime scene. Max scanned the dates; they were a month apart and began on a December in 1986. This jolted him out of his grogginess. *Is Desiderio Terran Rita Dolores? Is there a chance he's still alive, or at least has living relatives?* He checked the records on the address. It was a single family home in the name of Cesaria Terran, age 70. Phone records listed a number. A frail voice answered.

"Hello? Is this Mrs. Terran?"

"It's Mr. Terran, friend. Who's calling?"

Max nearly dropped the receiver. "Oh! I'm sorry sir, I...well, anyway it's you I was hoping to find."

"Well, friend, you found me."

"I believe we met, years ago. If I have the right person, that is... It was on the line at Bentley's?"

There was a pause, then the voice changed to a purr. "Is that my tall drink of water?"

"You remember me?"

"Oh, I don't forget tall, dark, and handsome."

"It's Max, yes. I'm a reporter now. I was wondering if you'd like to meet. I could drive over to see you."

"That would be delightful. You have the address, I take it."

The address led Max to a well-maintained split-ranch under mature maple trees. The next-door neighbor walking to his car eyed him suspiciously. Max gave him a wave and he turned away grouchily. He rang the bell and an old man cracked open the door. He was bald and frail, and wore thick-framed eyeglasses, but Max recognized his striking features even without all the makeup.

"There you are...thirst-quenching as ever! Though not such a wide-eyed innocent any more..."

"It's a pleasure to see you after all these years, ah..."

"Please, call me Desi," he said as he ushered Max into the front room.

"Desi. What a lovely home."

"I bought this house on sight. Something about the long view to the bay reminded me of Havana. I put it in my wife's name, due to complications…."

"I see." Max sensed that the word 'complications' was covering a lot. Desi guided him to a table in the bay window, set with tea service and sandwiches.

"She passed three years ago. She was a showgirl in Havana. *Una diosa de carne*, a flesh goddess, as they were called." He swept his hand at a wall of photos of his wife in elaborate outfits of sequins and feathers, onstage at the Tropicana Club.

"She was beautiful," Max said, examining the photos.

"She was exquisite. I was her dresser." He touched one of the photos. "Your next question. Yes, she knew."

"I see…" Max scrawled notes excitedly, wondering if he'd even be able to read them back to himself later.

"The police have been in touch with my old friend, the porter from the Aberdeen. A fellow *Habanero*. Still kicking at eighty-seven. He called me just before you did. It's been a busy morning…"

"I see. Do you think he will provide them with a lead?" Max asked.

"My old friend remembers little."

"Not unusual for a man his age."

Though he is otherwise very sharp," added Desi, sipping tea.

"Desi, I have to tell you something. I found something at the Aberdeen. It was overlooked during the investigation. Anyway, I picked it up…" Max placed the bandanna on the table and unfolded it to reveal the matchbook. Desi pursed his lips.

"That man, Jarvis? He had a complex. You must have learned by now that the world is full of men with complexes."

Taking notes, Max asked, "Was he your lover?"

"He was attracted to me…to Rita, but Rita is a lady," Desi said with a laugh.

"But you did know him?"

"Only as a fan," she answered, picking up a fan for effect. "But that night, he barged in on me while I was getting ready. I don't know how he found my room. I never gave him that," she said, pointing to the matchbook.

"When was this?"

"It was the one-year anniversary of the party. I performed Sarita's "Loca" in a full heartbreaker effect."

"Loca?" Max asked.

"*Loca, no saben lo que siento, ni que remordimiento, se oculta en mi interior…*" Desi sang. "I tried rejecting him politely, he was not my type at all, too short and angry."

"He didn't take it well?"

"He got violent with me. I could see him fumbling with a knife in his pocket. He threw himself at me, and I struck him in the head with my flask. Knocked him out cold."

"Did you call the police?"

"I returned to my dressing table. I had to get ready."

"Oh…"

"I thought he would sleep it off. I took his knife and went down for the show. I returned to my room after the party but the poor man was dead."

"But didn't you call the police then?"

"I did not like my chances of being believed…"

Desi ate a sandwich while Max stared into space. He imagined how the police back then would have responded to a call from a drag queen reporting a dead body. *They would see her illusion as lies*, he reckoned.

That last time he'd seen Rita flashed back at him, when she'd steered him away from that sketchy pusher with the mustache. For all of her lechery, she'd protected him.

"Desi, the coroner told me that the body was packed with mercury sulfide."

"The red powder? There were vials of it in his briefcase. I dumped them into the trunk and disposed of it separately."

"I see. Funny, it's thought to have a mummifying effect. The police believe it was used with intent."

"Well, that is an excellent theory," Desi mused. He gestured to the sandwiches and Max, suddenly finding himself very hungry, gulped down several.

"Abel Jarvis' wife told me she received money in an envelope after her husband's disappearance."

"My days at Bentley's were divine…" Desi answered in Rita's voice, then dropped a register: "Plus I got a good cut of the door."

"I see…" Max paused to take more notes. Desi finished a sandwich and wiped his mouth delicately, then leaned into the light.

"So, Max, you will write your blockbuster story," Desi stroked his bald head as if it held a glamorous mane. This frail man striking a pose was also the woman who had welcomed Max into her club. She'd made him cool, even desirable. Prior to that night, he'd always been turned down: too skinny, too dark, too geeky.

"You defended yourself—if what you're telling me is true."

"*Juro*," Desi said, raising his right hand.

"I believe you," said Max.

"But I let the man die so let's not paint me in a sympathetic light." As he looked down at his empty plate, a single tear tracked down his cheek.

"You couldn't have known," said Max. The autopsy had bolstered Ann's theory that Abel Jarvis had likely died from an aneurysm. If Max didn't like Rita's chance of being believed back then, he had his doubts about Desi's chance of being believed now.

"I'm going to discuss this with my boss," he said. Desi sighed. "But I won't let them railroad you."

"That's my tall drink of water," Desi said, managing a smile.

◆

"Whatcha got on the corpse in the trunk?" his boss asked upon Max's return to the newsroom.

"Your hunch was spot-on, boss. It's Abel Jarvis. The coroner confirmed it. I've got a connection there…" answered Max.

Max's boss tapped his head. "Hot damn, we got ourselves a scoop. What else?"

"The body was preserved with mercury sulfide, a chemical. From his own samples, apparently. He sold it for scientific and industrial uses, thermostats, barometers, also for dentistry…the cops are running down his co-workers, at least those still around. His wife had some ideas…"

"Get on this stat for tomorrow's edition, we drop the scoop, a twenty-year cold case mystery, the human interest angle," his boss enthused.

"I'm working one more lead, but need to tie up some loose ends…"

"Work on what you've got, we can follow it up," he interrupted.

Max exhaled. He hadn't held anything back and didn't have to write about Desi, though his boss had kept the door open to tell the whole story. The question was when? He focused on getting the story written and getting it to the editor.

Max's long-form story about the mysterious death of Abel Jarvis ran on the front page of the Saturday edition. Readers were drawn in by the gruesome circumstances:'LOCAL CHEMICAL SALESMAN MUMMIFIED IN HIS OWN SAMPLES,' as the headline put it. There was a hint of speculation, drawn from Linda's quotes, that he may have been killed by a jealous husband in the chemical field. Rita Delores, "an entertainer," was quoted as a regular hotel guest of the period to provide some background color. It was the top-selling edition in the paper's history and brought Max and his boss some shine.

That evening, Max went on the planned date with Burke and the two hit it off. Max had been a little put off by Burke's gruesome after-work wind-down talk, but beyond that found him decent and sincere. On their third date, Burke clocked Max for being distracted. Max confessed, "There's more to the Abel Jarvis case, I'm just not sure how to handle it…"

"Just go with your gut," said Burke, stopping him before he could say too much.

"Coming from you who knows all about guts…"

Ann Niebold stayed in touch, regularly hounding Max for intimate relationship details; Max would deflect. "I'll give you this, Ann. Burke does have an amazing ass," he said with a wink.

A week after the story dropped, Max's boss asked about that other lead he'd mentioned. He was eying a follow-up piece. Max answered, "Boss, can we go over it on Monday? There's something I have to do before it goes public." His boss shrugged in response.

That night, Burke and Max made their way to the Roseland Ballroom. Rita Dolores was making a return appearance to the stage for a GMHC benefit, prompted by her name appearing in Max's story. She was performing "Loca," just like she did the night of Abel Jarvis' demise. After the show, Burke and Max visited her backstage with a bouquet of roses.

"How kind of you." Rita air-kissed Max, then turned to Burke. "Are you taking care of my tall drink of water?" she asked, as she extended her hand.

"Oh, yes, ma'am," answered Burke. "The crowd loved you!"

"And now I know the song..." Max said.

"All of the emotions of that terrible encounter came back to me. I channeled them into my performance."

"You were..." Burke reached for a superlative. "...exquisite!"

"Thank you, dear." She turned to Max. "But how is your career? You are an eloquent writer. I shed a tear over the desolation of Linda Jarvis."

"My boss is thrilled. The story is bringing us both some positive attention..."

"Well, you've got success, you've got this beautiful man, why are you so sullen?"

"Oh, that's just how I am." Max answered. While Burke found a vase for the roses, he leaned in and whispered. "It's just that...my boss wants more..."

"Then you must write the full story. I don't have much time left in any case..."

"Oh stop," Max replied. "I don't know, I could go in tomorrow and tell him my lead didn't pan out.'

"Would you really do that?"

"I'm torn. The story is incomplete, but I don't want them to drag you in..."

"*Drag?* I am a woman," said Rita, drawing a circle around her mug.

"You know what I mean. It's...uncomfortable sitting on a secret..."

"Ha!" Rita leaned back, outlined her perfectly made-up face with an elongated hand, continuing the motion to caress her sequined gown, then snapped her fan. "Welcome to my world."

TRAUMATIC BOOK REVIEW: *ALIVE*, BY PIERS PAUL READ

"We are born without shame!" yelled a man at the edge of town, naked except for hiking boots and sunglasses, holding a sign with a red slash through some numbers.

Vin didn't know that the good people of Vermont had endorsed nudity—as a matter of policy, if not as individual lifestyle—until he arrived in Brattleboro. Maybe it was one reason Shaw and his lover chose the state for summer getaways? He'd boarded the Vermonter at Penn Station and rode the steady train up as it tracked the Connecticut River. For much of the ride, he squatted in the café car. He'd developed the habit of traveling with an emergency stash, anticipating a derailment, extreme flooding, or some unforeseen calamity: granola bars, jerky, mixed nuts, chocolates, sugar packets, bandages, aspirin, matches, nips of whiskey. He broke open the chocolates and shared them with other passengers to start up conversations, hoping to be suitably socialized for the weekend ahead, to be spent in close quarters with Shaw, his lover, and their other guests.

Vin was met at the station by a young man named Oz, a college student who worked at the food co-op and tended the couple's kitchen garden in their absence. He was standing next to a shiny new hybrid, craning over the exiting crowd. He had a wide smile, brown clay skin, and something lupine in the brow. It was on the ride to the house that they passed the nudist with the sign, and that sure did break the ice.

"There's no state law against it…only some local ordinances, which he seems to be contesting. It's legal to be naked in public as long as you're not being lewd," explained Oz.

"Live free or die, I guess," Vin replied.

"Well, that's the next state over, but in the same spirit."

Oz chatted about his affiliation with the nearby Radical Faerie encampment called Destiny and his hikes to Rock River, where people skinny-dipped. On a slow stretch, he smiled and locked eyes with Vin, who was spellbound by the effect of his irises glimmering with reflections of passing foliage. He then fixated on Oz's feet as they flexed in flip-flops to accelerate and brake. His toenails were painted a deep red color which on the little bottle rattling in the cup holder was labeled oxblood.

They stopped at the garden, which lay behind two cherry trees, their intertwined boughs heavy with pulpy drupes. Oz showed off the neat rows of vegetables and a raised bed fragrant with herbs. "How beautiful," uttered Vin, overwhelmed at the sight of this tidy plot, thinking about the care that Oz put into it. Oz took the opportunity to flirt: "You're so handsome. I love your salt and pepper," he said as he reached to stroke Vin's beard. Vin's cheeks flushed to the color of chard stalk, and he replied with a mumbled "That's nice of you, Oz," to which he countered: "I'm not being nice! Shaw guessed I'd be attracted to you, and he was right." He flushed again.

Vin thought of Shaw as a frenemy. They'd known each other since they were young men on the prowl on Fire Island and had a checkered history. Shaw was a striking blonde who was abandoned by his mother at a young age and raised by a foster family. He'd thrown himself into gymnastics, and his combination of good looks and athleticism dazzled the homeowner set. Vin was Long Island guido trade, an attractive local boy, just rough enough around the edges. They made a good team because they didn't compete for the same men. Perhaps because of his upbringing, Shaw had always been emotionally impenetrable, a trait Vin found infuriating. Over the years, he'd periodically let the friendship lapse for this reason.

"So you and Shaw go back a long way?" asked Oz as they walked to the car.

"Since the days on Fire Island."

He and Shaw were the only survivors of that circle. Mac, the record collector who deejayed all their gatherings, died in the hospital after a bout of meningitis. Christos, who grew their weed in his Brooklyn backyard, scoffed at conventional treatments and had a heart attack while on a vision quest on Zuni land. Irresistible Javier, whom they called el lobo, threw himself off the George Washington bridge rather than face his decline. He may well have survived in time for antiretrovirals. The memories Vin and Shaw shared of this group, golden under the Fire Island sun, were usually what prompted Vin to renew contact with Shaw after each lapse.

This time it was the publication of Vin's novella had brought them back in touch. A small imprint had recently released his veiled account of his experiences as the lover of an older writer, a "doyen of gay literature," as the blurb put it. Vin had sent Shaw a copy since he appeared in one chapter. He was the one person for whom Vin did not have to invent a pseudonym; Shaw had legally changed his name some years ago so Vin just used his old one. The gift had rekindled their friendship once more and Shaw had invited him up for the weekend. The cottage belonged to Shaw's lover, Warner, a college professor he also found emotionally impenetrable.

The silent-running hybrid crunched up the gravel driveway. Everyone except Warner was out. He gave the new arrival a tour and laid out the weekend's guest list. The cottage was a restored saltbox with a deep front porch. Helen, a colleague of Warner's in the Gender and Sexuality program, was in one of the guest rooms. Vin had the other guest room, and two of Shaw's friends were roughing it in a converted shed. "That's Wantastiquet Mountain through your window," Warner noted of the view.

The wide-planked heart pine floors showed the wear of two centuries. Warner's flat tone modulated only when they reached the room opposite the kitchen: "And this is our library," he said with a flourish. The walls were lined with bookshelves from floor to ceiling, breaking only for doorways and windows. The sweet, melting aroma of a baking pie wafted in. A central table held art books and ephemera, and stacks of paperbacks surfaced from the floor like stalagmites. Plush armchairs were tucked into the corners, each with its own reading lamp.

Shaw and the other guests returned from the swimming hole, toweled and glowing, bearing a faint odor of minerals and algae. After introductions, the swimmers retreated to dress. Their return was a pageant of scanty attire, as none deigned to wear much that hot evening, just enough to avoid trouble in the kitchen. A gauzy langot here, a jockstrap/tank top combo there, and the winner, by universal acclaim, was Shaw in spangled booty shorts. Vin suddenly felt overdressed. After an impromptu runway on the porch, the group gathered in the dining room for a pot luck.

Vin had brought some lard bread from an Italian bakery in Brooklyn. It was set on the table with the other dishes, prompting Shaw to announce, "This is made with pig, for the vegetarians," eliciting pursed frowns from several guests. The others presented their respective dishes with some fanfare and a line formed. The group broke off into their subsets; Vin found himself paired with Helen.

After wiping out the dinner everyone made their way to the library. The armchairs were all spoken for so Vin took a spot on the floor, laying on a pillow, pulling his t-shirt down over his belly. Someone's damp dog settled next to him, and Oz lay down with his head on his thighs. He pulled a paperback off the top of the nearest stack.

"*Alive*, the story of the Andean survivors," Oz read off the cover, which featured a photo of a jagged, snowy peak.

"Omigod, I read that when I was a kid," and as Vin took it from him, a surge of recollection hit.

"You must have been quite the reader."

""My dad brought it home one day..." He spread its yellowed pages. "Surprising, because he wasn't much of a reader. I think someone at the office lent it to him. His engineer's mind must have enjoyed puzzling out the challenges of the survivors. I snuck it out of his room while he was at work..."

"That's dedication," said Oz.

"Here's the part where they're rescued: 'Then, before Serda returned, they took what remained of the human flesh they had brought with them and buried it under a stone...'"

"Hello...spoiler alert!"

"Sorry!" said Vin, yet he kept reading: "'...for no sooner had the bread and cheese passed their lips than some of the early revulsion they had felt returned to them.'"

"How old were you when you read that?"

Vin checked the publication date and tallied: "Twelve..."

Surmising he was not getting *Alive* back any time soon, Oz found Warner's famous article from a few years back, in which he argued that the political fight for gay marriage has had a detrimental, normalizing effect on queer culture.

Vin scoured the pages of *Alive*, seeking an entry point. He gulped over the part when the survivors of the crash–Uruguayan rugby players stranded in a broken fuselage up on a barren mountain–eat the frozen buttock of one of their teammates, who was among the first to perish. Though newly immersed in the fate of the team, he found himself sinking into a digestive coma. He'd gone in for seconds of Helen's mac and cheese. His head slumped before the survivors started eying the wounded.

Warner nudged him awake with a bare foot; he looked around to find the library empty. Noting the paperback on his chest, he smiled. "*Alive*. Who knows how that turned up here? Guests in and out, someone must have left it behind…"

Vin roused. "One of the survivors–Canessa–was my first crush."

"Ah! Now we know. You're into jock cannibal trade," Warner joked, as he gave him a hand up.

Morning broke and bright sun roused everyone from their deep slumber. The household assembled for breakfast.

"What's up for today?"

"Back to the swimming hole! Vin hasn't seen it."

"We're checking out an estate sale," said Shaw's friend Tolly. The remaining guests assembled after breakfast for the hike to the swimming hole.

"And Oz?" Vin asked, noting his absence.

"He has work today. He'll probably be back tomorrow," Shaw answered with a smile.

Vin prepared a picnic for the excursion. He found bread and a wheel of local cheese, and packed them in a little-used basket, along with some fruit. It was about a two mile hike, through Warner's property, then crossing the road and down a rocky hillside. He struggled with the basket as they scrambled through scree.

"Watch where you put your hands," yelled Warner. "Rattlers under the rocks."

He made it to the swimming hole uninjured. The flat rock at the water's edge had warmed with the morning sun. They staked their claims and shed their clothes. Warner kept his hiking shoes on and wore a visor. Shaw had only an iPod strapped to his bicep and headphones. Helen's fanny pack served as a fig leaf. Vin fumbled with his shorts, hesitant to remove them. Although he'd attained peak fitness here and there, he'd gotten thick in the middle lately, while Shaw's mysterious illness had kept him lean through the years, if not in the athletic form of his youth.

Shaw hopped onto an island rock and dangled his legs in the water while listening to music while the others warmed their bodies on the ledge. Just as Vin summoned the courage to remove his shorts, Shaw started singing along to his iPod. He never had a great voice, but his enthusiasm was endearing. "I just can't get enough/must have seconds of love..." was the refrain he sang over and over. Even if it had nothing to do with Vin's body—Shaw wasn't even looking his way—he couldn't help but feel targeted. His shorts were already off but he kept his tee shirt on and lay against the rock, already demoralized.

"You shirt-cocking today, Vin?" asked Shaw. Vin gave a puzzled look.

"Isn't that a Burner thing?" Helen asked.

"Right, just trying not to burn," Vin answered.

Vin was astounded at how little they ate. They slurped on the peaches and plums, ignoring the rest.

"Oz brought those from the co-op," Shaw said of the stone fruit.

"Perfectly ripe—even the bruises taste good," answered Vin. He devoured the remaining fruit, thinking of Oz. He smeared the softening cheese onto bread with his pocket knife, but having no takers, stuffed it all himself.

Upon their return, Vin sought out a quiet spot where he could tuck into *Alive*. He tried the front porch, but found Helen had already claimed it. She was immersed in reading a novel called *The Uninvited Guests*. After an awkward moment she looked up and smiled, tapping the empty rocker next to hers.

"You know I met your late lover, he was a visiting lecturer..."

"Oh?"

"He was a handful."

"Ha! He was grouchy. He'd complain about it, but secretly loved the attention from academics..." Vin turned solemn. "Honestly, Helen, when he died, I felt some relief. Our last year was...difficult. But times like this, I miss him so much. We'd have laughed together at the silliness. Without him..."

"That's funny, he told me he missed you being there. Said you usually came along on his lecture dates, kept him laughing at us academics..."

They locked eyes and smiled. "Thank you for reminding me," Vin said, opening *Alive* as Helen returned to her reading.

The following morning was unusually hot; the cooler air that typically settled into their valley overnight had circulated elsewhere. The guests wore even less than usual, and Vin opted for a tank top he wasn't entirely sure about. Oz returned to the house, squeezing his shoulder as he passed him on his way to the kitchen. "Don't let them burn today," he said.

"It's a perfect day for Rock River! Oz, you take Helen and Vin in the hybrid, we'll take the jeep," said Shaw.

The assembled group hiked along the river; recent flooding had knocked out a part of the trail, making for some perilous grappling. Safely in the gay area, the group stripped out of their clothes and frolicked under the dappled sunlight. Vin backed away from the river, settling under a tree along the upper bank.

A passel of near-naked hikers—to a man lean paragons of fitness—descended upon Vin on their way up the trail, causing him to sit up and take notice. A few minutes later, a young straggler from the group sauntered by, smiling. He wore a bandanna around his neck, a red triangle pointing downward towards his carved, downy six-pack. Fear rummaged through Vin's forebrain at the sight of it. Shaw, having spotted the attractive straggler, leapt off his rock and scrambled up the ledge.

Shaw engaged the young man in the most perfunctory conversation before copping a feel of his hefty package, displaying it to Vin as if a prize. The straggler grinned, then led Shaw into the wood. Vin sunk back on his towel. All those days at the beach, his thickness had been compared to Shaw's gymnastic perfection. Though this pebbly spit was no Fire Island, here they were again. He hadn't anticipated reliving those days when he'd agreed to travel to Vermont, and his ill-preparedness made him shudder.

Shaw emerged from the wood, sweaty and tumescent. He made a show of wiping his mouth and licking his fingers. "Delicious," he said with a teasing grin, as he tossed off his iPod and jumped into the river. The others took his cue and jumped in after him, leaving Vin to simmer.

Back in his room, Vin packed his clothing and squirreled away his emergency stash, refreshed with a few items stolen from the pantry. He was confirming his train reservation when Oz walked in, carrying a slim book in his hand. It looked like his own novella, the copy he'd sent to Shaw; Oz noticed him squinting at the cover. "*The Chronicler's Lover*, by Dom Vincent," he read the title, and then from one of the blurbs: "...an enjoyably grubby read for the astute fan." Vin winced. He'd published it under a pseudonym, due to legal challenges from his dead lover's agent, and wasn't sure if Oz would connect him to it.

"I'm still re-reading *Alive*," Vin said, holding up the paperback.

"Ah, your jock cannibal boyfriend," Oz said. He must have heard that from Warner. Oz moved his suitcase off the bed so he could spread out next to him. They got some reading time in before they were called down for dinner, keeping the slightest contact between their warm bodies: Vin mapping the arch of Oz's foot with his toes, Oz stretching his arm out to caress his beard.

A ratatouille made from the garden bounty, topped with cheese from a neighbor's dairy, and a fresh cornbread hit the table. There was much praise for those who grew the vegetables, and for Warner, the cook, too. Helen gave a blessing: "Goddess, we gather together to nourish our bodies and celebrate our abundance. Blessings upon the food and drink we share." The guests responded with enthusiastic shouts of "Blessed be!"

Hungry from the day at Rock River, they emptied every bowl. The wine flowed. Warner's exquisite pie, the crust buttery, the cherries tart, culminated this locavore feast. Even the last of the lard bread was consumed. Conversation was lively and covered a range of topics, from gardening to radical queer politics to an upcoming Faerie gathering.

Shaw had drunk his share of wine when the topic of body types came up: "I love everyone, twinks, bears, otters, muscle..."

"Oh, I'd fancy a hairy muscle man, just once," said Helen with a laugh.

"It's not like I even agree with it, but these terms get thrown around the office," Shaw dodged. Shaw was the CEO of rentboy.com, a listing service for male escorts. His job scandalized Warner's academic colleagues, to Warner's great delight. "For instance, Oz is a muscle pup," he said. Oz's brow creased skeptically. Though Shaw had just denied the value of such typology, he went on to profile each of his guests: "Rubén is a twink, Tolly is a daddy." Then he turned to Vin, with a pause: "You're totally not a bear, but not quite a jock either. Maybe if you stripped down..."

Vin shot him a look that reached back to the Eighties. He'd always been oblivious to the weight of his words. Back then he just didn't talk that much, except when wine loosened him up, like now. How they were mesmerized by him: the blond, blue-eyed orphan boy, this masculine ideal. They were so dumbstruck by his appearance that he'd had little occasion to develop social nuance.

Vin's hurt was evident to almost everyone. It was awful to have a non-conforming part of you set out publicly, apologetically, like a fallen soufflé.

Oz jumped in to defend him: "I like a man with a little meat on his bones!"

"I thought you were vegetarian," deadpanned Warner, seeking to lighten the mood.

Vin mouthed a "thank you" to Oz, amid laughter. "I'm going for aged-out guido in roomy tracksuits," he joked, to more laughter than it deserved. "Really though, do we have to commodify each other, market ourselves like products? Can't I just live in my body?" Vin leveled a look at Shaw, who was throwing back more wine, oblivious as ever, but Warner was nodding his head in agreement. It was nice to have a potent—if silent—ally. This awkwardness ended the dinner conversation, and the group drifted into the library.

Vin claimed a chair this time and settled into it with *Alive*, while Oz sat on the floor, leaning against his legs. He recalled, after sneaking it out of his dad's nightstand and finishing it in one sitting, eating robustly where he once picked indifferently, while at the same time repulsed by the quantities of meat on display at Sunday dinners. He remembered crushing on Canessa, the hefty pragmatist. Humiliating incidents from his sexual awakening, fraught as it was with its own jagged perils, flashed in his mind; then the fates of the sturdy young men from a pleasant, abundant land, having success as a team, traveling the continent surrounded by loved ones and supporters. Somnolence again overwhelmed his desire to revisit the sorrowful story and its effects. His eyes crossed and fluttered at every return.

Oz shook him gently: "You were mumbling…Canessa? Old Christians? Do you want to go to bed?"

"Yeah, I'm beat," said Vin as he roused from his stupor. Oz gave him a hand out of the chair; he was stronger than he looked.

"I'm enjoying your book," Oz said, grinning. On the way upstairs, Vin invited him to share his bed. Maybe because he was so tired, he just came out and asked without hedging. Oz happily agreed. Vin let him into his room and stumbled towards the bathroom. On the way, he saw Helen down the corridor. She was wearing nothing but panties, one arm was folded over her breasts, and her flesh joggled with every soft footfall. Her body was luminous and ripe in the incidental light, and a spasm of emotion overwhelmed Vin at the sight of her shuffling away. Tears welled as he stood in awe of her fulsomeness. He missed the warm folds of his dead lover. He gulped the night air as she disappeared behind the door.

He wiped his face on his shirt and, avoiding the mirror like a morose vampire, brushed his teeth in his reflection in the window. Wantastiquet Mountain was settling into midnight, a low mound silently hovering over the tree line.

Back in his room, he found Oz stripping down to an adorable pair of briefs with a Keith Haring print. He had sturdy legs and a compact ass. Stripped of his defenses, Vin exclaimed, "O, wolf-boy!"

Oz gave him a wink and mugged wolfishly. Vin winked back, then Oz removed his shirt. The hardness of his contours brought back that long-standing revulsion.

"Everything okay?" asked Oz.

He'd noticed that Vin had turned slightly green. He had no visible fat stores, though Vin had watched him eat heartily. How could he trust such a ruthless metabolism?

"Uh, yeah... I was dreaming about *Alive*. It left a big impression. Maybe I was too young. It made me fear starvation. Probably just a silly excuse for years of emotional eating. The sight of a lean body..."

"Are you afraid of me?" Oz smiled, and ran a hand along his clavicle.

For years, his self-image had been informed by this irrational arc. This fear had colonized his relationship to food and men. Oz awaited an answer, but Vin hesitated. The Old Christians gave of themselves to their brothers. Brave Oz desired him without judgment, and deserved love. He was a gardener, associated with bounty, and his camping skills might come in handy.

"Promise not to eat me if we get stranded on a mountain," Vin demanded. Oz laughed.

"I'm vegetarian, remember?"

"And you'll hike down with me?"

"We'll save the team!" replied Oz, as he reached for his beard.

That night in the free state of Vermont, Vin released his stubborn, ingrown fear. He shed his clothes and let his soft middle just be, exhaling like it was the first time. Oz gave an approving look, and Vin ran a tremulous hand along his ridged trunk: his rectus, his serratus, his oblique, his iliac furrow. Then they went down that mountain to rescue.

THE MARIELITO

"The exile is a person who, having lost a loved one, keeps searching for the face he loves in every new face and, forever deceiving himself, thinks he has found it."

—Reinaldo Arenas

I met him in the Central Park Ramble as night relieved the heaviness of summer heat. It was ten-thirty by my new Casio. He approached while I was having a smoke in the Rustic Shelter, fixing on me with his pooled-chocolate eyes, pouting, then shyly laying his head upon my shoulder. He said something to me in Spanish which I didn't catch, so I asked him to repeat it: "*¿Pero qué haces aquí, Capitán?*"

What was I doing there? I'd stalked the winding paths of the city's wild woodland garden for hours, running into friends under the lamplight, diverging into hideaways here and there. Back then in the eighties, the Ramble by night was our vast, marvelous cruising ground. We'd come from all over the city—all over the world really—on word of mouth, on coded whispers. We didn't have apps to locate each other; we had our noses. There we could still ping each other through space. The cops sometimes patrolled but at least it wasn't a data mining operation.

This master of the shy pick-up took me to his railroad flat in Hell's Kitchen. The narrow space was full of plants, like some greenhouse annex of the Park. They ripened the air with oxygen, most welcome after climbing all those stairs, and seemed to spread as I waited by the door while he moved some bags off the bed.

When he told me he was from Havana, I asked when he'd arrived. His answer, "Nineteen Eighty," prompted me to tell him about my high school obsession with Blondie. I tried to explain the battle between disco and rock, how I'd been called *faggot* for liking the band, but the story didn't seem to land. He began telling me his story—his passage on the Mariel Boatlift, that flotilla of undesirables—reluctantly at first, mainly to put a stop to my nervous chatter.

"I was sent to prison for falling in love with a classmate. Fausto had the head of a puma, and he loved me back. His mother reported me for corrupting her son, that's what I heard. He was only a little younger. His skin was lighter than mine, we say *un jabao lindo*. We never did anything but kiss."

He kissed me, chastely, to demonstrate their intimacy. He blinked slowly so his long lashes brushed my cheeks.

"That was our sex."

I took his head in my hands, my fingers rummaging through his soft brown curls. I thought we'd kiss again, but he had more to say:

"The prison was full of homosexuals, Capitán. We re-made a whole society for ourselves, one little act of flamboyance at a time. It was our currency. After my release, I heard about the asylum seekers. It was Fausto's uncle who drove me to the Peruvian Embassy and bribed the guard. I never saw Fausto again."

He slipped from my hold to prepare some tea from his mint plant. We talked until the airshaft glowed with soft dawn and the neighbor turned on her radio. We fucked tenderly, our percussion keeping time with the music, and after, he offered me breakfast. As I took the last bite of toast, dipped in cafe con leche the way he'd insisted, he whispered to a plant with dark leaves and pink flowers. He caught me looking.

"She is Adelfa, my faithful companion in here La Yuma. That's what Cubans say, but I prefer the name my Mexican brothers give it: Gringolandia."

Over the years, we'd occasionally run into each other in the Ramble. He resisted getting a mobile phone but eventually gave in. His texts were curt and coded. He stopped calling me Capitán: "You once reminded me of Ahab in *Moby-Dick* but not any more." He'd watched the film as a child at a contraband screening. I did have unruly hair and a beard back then. Instead, he switched to calling me Puma:

"Puma, do you still have your hair?"

"Puma, I have nothing here but my sorrow."

There were days when I thought he was outright mistaking me for Fausto, and others when I thought that his memories of Cuba had fused with those of our first encounter. He sent greetings from his plants Adelfa and Hierbabuena, among others. He was deeply suspicious of electronic surveillance. He'd explained that during his time under Castro, rewarding denunciations to maintain social cohesion and revolutionary aims was the norm. When I stopped going to the Ramble—our cruising ground had lately been swept by police, plus everyone was starting to cruise online—we kept in touch intermittently.

The long, hot nights of another summer and a pinch of nostalgia returned my thoughts to the Marielito, his furrowed brow, his thick hands. I hadn't heard from him in over a year and was seized with a grim thought. Looking up Adelfa in the Spanish-English dictionary, I learned that she is oleander, a common but poisonous shrub: *Can cause death if ingested, as in a tea.* I texted him but got no response. I headed towards his building, walking briskly through the park, my anxiety mounting. As I approached Columbus Circle, passing the Maine Monument—which coincidentally commemorates a U.S. battleship blown up in Havana harbor—a man in a Parks Department uniform yelled: "Puma! You've gone gray."

The Marielito rose from his work in the soil and removed his safari hat. Slick tears coated my cheeks.

"Puma, look what they have me doing, I'm nourishing roots, me..." he said, pointing to the mulched soil.

"That's lovely," I said, wiping my face. "You look well..."

"I'm strong, eh Puma?" He removed his work gloves.

"Yes, you fit right in here...."

He sang out a song I could not follow, which he read in my searching eyes.

"I bring Abrecaminos for your destiny," he half-translated.

"...And how is Adelfa?"

"Ah, you know, Puma." I nodded. "She's a bit down, can you imagine? Jealous of my new life..." He wiped my face with his warm hand. "She's always been dramatic, but faithful."

SATELLITE RULES, STRANDED LONGINGS

Upon being dropped off at the budget hotel, its blinky sign pulsing over an empty parking lot, Dave had a hard time believing it was centrally located as advertised, though it hulked very near to the confluence of three rivers, the locus of Milwaukee. Once inside the dusty plastic flowers exhibit that was the lobby, he doubted that flush, name-tagged Kimmy could summon cheer without narcotics. Dave had had a long day at the Convention Center.

Dave was in town for a Harley trade show because—through little agency of his own—he was a sales rep for several licensed products, including protective goggles and sunglasses. His cousin had done the job for thirty years until a heart attack knocked him off his bike. Dave focused on the public good of it. He made bikers a little safer. He'd gotten to know the shapes and sizes of their heads, the curvature of their brows. It was a kind of intimacy, a way of caring for others. He'd put on his best impression of a motorcycle aficionado and earnestly sell them on the products. Truth be told, he was a New York homosexual who liked his quiet, and whose preference for two-wheeled locomotion involved no motor, just a nice bell.

So he'd make the annual trek to some American city with adequate convention facilities to meet with his accounts, the merchandise managers of dealerships in the Northeast. Most of the dealerships were run by aged-out boomers. It was the same with the sales force, all men in their sixties clinging to misspent youths. At forty-seven, Dave was the youngest rep on the national team, so he was welcomed as a shot of fresh blood—though not without raising some eyebrows. He spent the first day of the trade show maintaining the charade while checking out the few hot guys in attendance—mostly the grown sons of owners who'd taken up the family business. All day he'd scoped these sturdy, well-fed young men and how they filled their jeans. They'd occasionally catch him and return the most oblivious smiles.

On a break at the coffee station—in a corner where no one could see his phone screen—Dave opened the app. It was his preferred of several mobile platforms for male-on-male cruising. He wanted to see if anyone else at the show was stealth like him. None of the sturdy sons were there. A few brown-skinned guys showed non-identifiable parts of themselves—probably waiters from the dining hall.

Once Dave got settled in his hotel room the app started pinging. He was happily surprised to note several promising pings from not too far off. Living in New York, he was accustomed to pings from close proximities. In the grid of prospects, some were in the same building, some next door. Others were on the next block, but in the back of the building, separated by only a hundred and some odd feet, two exterior walls, and a chasm of rear space. In Milwaukee, distances were measured in miles.

Dave would have gladly walked a few miles to break through the strangeness and share pleasure with someone, or they could come to the hotel if they could get past Kimmy. It said right there in the Bible in the nightstand, 'love thy neighbor,' and with the help of the satellite array encircling in medium Earth orbit, transmitting location data into his pocket, that was the plan.

He checked out this guy only 1.4 miles away. The guy was smiling in his photo; that was a good sign. Dave did not appreciate scowlers. The smiler had dark hair and eyes and a somewhat large forehead. Dave found him compelling in an otherworldly way, plus he had a sense of humor. His name was also Dave and they joked about that. The Daves exchanged some photos, first candids, then more intimate shots, like a flip-book striptease. Other Dave looked squat and sturdy, although maybe there was some distortion going on in the mirror shots he sent? They complimented each other and asked the 'host or travel' question; Other Dave specified that he'd prefer company. This suited Dave just fine as it was a clear night and he wanted to get out after a day spent in a forced-air environment.

Dave prepared to break out of isolation, take a nice urban hike, and love his neighbor. He mentally rehearsed a sequence of actions–getting Other Dave's address, mapping the location, determining the best walking path, brushing his teeth, fixing his hair, changing out of his work shirt–when Other Dave messaged him: 'So you're ok with me being dwarf?' To which he added the bicep, mouse, and winking man emojis. He felt a flush of embarrassment, which was a weird thing to feel alone in a room. He checked Other Dave's stats, and sure enough, his height was listed as 4'-9", on the tall side for a dwarf, as Dave learned from the results of a hasty dive into search engines. An image flashed of a porn he once came across, a bull-like, street-tough dwarf fucking two full-sized girls. His mind searched for any real-life interactions with dwarves and came up blank.

Dave had once hooked up with a guy with flippers for arms, a thalidomide baby. Don with the flippers was handsome and owned a brownstone in Chelsea. Dave was surprised when he opened the door since Don had not shared his circumstance with him. Right there on the stoop, he understood the photo cropping decisions Don had made. He imagined all the men in his situation who turned around and ran back down the steps, and right there decided he did not want to be one of them. Don had a serious scowl. Dave gave him his ass because he couldn't give him arms, riding him while holding on to his shoulders.

Dave hooked up with a Wolf Man in Boston, who'd lost an arm after a drunken motorcycle accident. They sat next to each other at an AA meeting, and afterwards made out in Wolf Man's pick-up truck. He had a sense-memory of the electrical discharge that ran up his arm when Wolf Man gently touched him with his mechanical claw prosthetic. Recalling these past encounters, Dave hesitated to meet up with Other Dave just because of his dwarfism. That would be exploitation—but then he remembered that he'd been attracted to Other Dave before he even knew. He found himself replying: 'Yes I am cool.'

Dave took all the steps he anticipated taking in preparing to meet Other Dave. The path he'd mapped took him across the Menomonee River along 6th Street; its cable-stayed bridge hummed in the night. He walked past the vast museum—where he would later spend a morning feigning interest—and into Walker's Point. At .7 miles, an angry drunk stumbled out of a Mexican place called Conejito's, breaking the solitary spell. Up until then Milwaukee had given the night to him alone. He wondered if Other Dave was a furious rabbit.

The app showed smaller distances between active users as Dave advanced on Other Dave's address, leading him to surmise he was in a gay neighborhood. Other Dave lived on a block of working-class houses, outside of a looming factory complex with a clock tower. It was modest wooden structure with shabby asphalt roof tiles and a projecting front porch. The steps creaked under his feet, and Other Dave appeared at the window, smiling, even before he had a chance to knock. He must have been tracking his approach on the app.

"Hello! Welcome to Milwaukee," said Other Dave in full voice, and as they shook hands, he pulled Dave in for a hug. He burnished his large forehead against Dave's chest which Dave found arousing, but once the hug was over, Dave felt at loose ends. He didn't know what to say or how to move.

Other Dave led Dave in and invited him to sit on a full-sized recliner, while he sprawled on the low sofa, which was a standard size but with the feet removed. The Daves had a nice chat; Other Dave worked at that factory complex down the street. He was an engineer developing automation processes for manufacturing. Dave told Other Dave about his work among the bikers and how that came to be. Other Dave explained how his interest in robotics emerged from trying to solve the problems of access in a full-sized world. Then he mentioned that he used to dance shirtless on a bar, pouring shots for straight crowds, to put himself through engineering school, and Dave got really aroused.

Their sexual attraction was palpable. Dave was turned on by Other Dave's compact musculature and the size of his forehead. His brow was broad and flat and perfect in its way, and Dave longed to touch it with his eyes closed, to snug it like a pair of extra large goggles. The kindness in Dave's eyes brought out a dominant streak in Other Dave, who felt an urge to make this full-sizer submit rising in him.

They moved into the bedroom, and Dave tried something he'd been thinking about: he got on his knees and nuzzled into Other Dave's chest, just the way Other Dave did at the front door. Dave felt Other Dave's arousal through his pants. They removed their shirts; Dave inhaled of Other Dave's armpits and licked a nipple. Dave admired Other

Dave's muscular arms, although he saw something baby-like about the proportions. With Dave kneeling before him, Other Dave silently took charge.

Other Dave ordered Dave to undress with a stern look, then pushed him down into a cross-legged position. He reached back in time for some of his bar-top stripper moves, and gave Dave a slow striptease to his briefs. He said while gyrating, "You know, Dave, if it weren't for out-of-towners I'd never get laid. The locals treat me like a pet." Then he pushed his crotch into Dave's face.

When they lay down together on Dave's low bed. The height difference melted away but not the power dynamic. Once they found each others' triggers, Other Dave crawled on top of Dave and lay on him like a pool raft. They stayed like that for a long while, glued together by their commingled spunk, all difference fused away.

Other Dave offered to take Dave out to dinner if they could agree on a night. Dave initially believed it was a sincere offer before spasming with doubt. He decided instead it was a polite sendoff and returned to his hotel a different way because he didn't like to backtrack. The return walk took him right by the Confluence, where he entertained the notion that tonight a GPS satellite was passing right overhead. GPS had been invented by the government for military and navigational purposes yet here he was applying it to his longing for intimacy. Currents of aggression, exploitation, and lust ran along the same channel, he mused. "That's confluence," he found himself saying aloud as he craned to face the moon.

After another airless day of sales rites in the Convention Center, Dave walked the trail along the banks of the Milwaukee River, crossing bridge after bridge. It was a warm evening and the city's waterways were buzzing with locals on leisurely outings in pleasure boats. The app came to life as he cut through various neighborhoods, mapping trajectories as men left their jobs and sought each other out.

Dave came to life too, breathing briny air and seeing new things, remembering fondly his encounter with Other Dave. At least his airless day had been a good one for sales. He hesitated to acknowledge his specific longings, but after last night, he wanted to stand head-to-head with a man and not feel *that* awkwardness. He'd remember to review all stats that night.

He ran into two of his associates and they cajoled him into dining together at a riverfront brewpub. They exchanged war stories from the day—tales of difficult buyers and big sales that got away—over brats and pale ales. At a pause in the background clatter of the establishment, Dave's colleagues heard the distinctive ping of the app coming from his phone, and confused looks cut across their table. He was usually so careful to silence his phone around work colleagues.

He left them to their last round of ale and checked in with the app. One of the pings seemed promising, although it was from seven miles away. His screen name was Victor, also a good sign. Dave liked when app men went by their names, not some invented handle boasting of prowess or staking a claim on a sexual position. Victor reported that he was just finishing work and needed to travel.

Victor was twenty-five, tall, good-looking. Dave had grown accustomed to attention from younger guys; he didn't especially like being called 'daddy,' but was grateful that they called him at all. At least Victor hadn't used that word. Victor appeared in his profile photo in a bright blue t-shirt, and the background is all glossy white brightness recognizable as an Apple Store interior. Dave twitched with lust over the prospect of hooking up with a guy from the Genius Bar.

Dave had a back catalog of delectable fantasies about ravaging the nerdy-hot tech guys he'd encountered in Apple Stores. He couldn't help mentioning to Victor that he'd been an Apple fan since the days of the Mac Classic, with the 9-inch mono-chrome screen and 4 MB of memory. That was when he first started hooking up with men, through the America Online chat rooms. Perhaps this was an overshare on Dave's part. Victor told Dave about his preference for older guys, mainly because they were nice to him. Most guys his age were way too self-absorbed, or indifferent, or mean. Victor offered to meet him at his hotel in about an hour. He'd take the bus from Wauwatosa.

Victor arrived at the hotel after the long trip, the blue dash of his bus having lurched through hundreds of faster dots. He was friendly and talkative, yet Dave detected an air of sadness. It was later than expected and Dave struggled to keep alert for Victor's chatter. Victor said he like working at the Genius Bar and didn't mind taking the late shifts like he had that night. Dave sensed that Victor talked about work so much to avoid other subjects. Finally Dave and Victor hit the bed and it was like a married couple enacting their routine.

Dave was smitten with Victor's smooth brown skin, his lean frame, his meaty ass. Victor whispered to Dave: "I'd like to stay the night, is that okay?" His voice trembled and Dave sensed that Victor felt safer with him—a stranger—than at home. Maybe he liked being in a random hotel room where no one could track him. He had turned off his phone. The strangers had a romantic night, hours of kissing and grinding. As dawn light leaked between the vertical blinds, Victor lifted his legs for Dave, who fucked a stubborn nut out of him. Between the conversation and the slow-burning sex, they'd been up for hours and Dave was completely spent. Even with a tired smile on Victor's face, the dark brown dots of his eyes looked miles away, further than the unseen Canadian shore of Lake Michigan. Dave had hoped to sex the sadness out of him but apparently not. Victor slept nestled into him. After a few hours, the alarm sounded and Dave dressed as silently as he could manage. He left Victor sleeping as he made his way towards his final day of capitalist frenzy.

Dave zombie-walked through that morning. On his break he ran over to the coffee bar to throw back a Red Eye and check the app. He was scheduled to leave the next day, and that night he'd sleep, so there was really no reason; it had just become reflexive. Dave found a new guy who went by 'Swingl' just 51 feet away. Otherwise it was mostly the same array of faceless brown body parts. Swingl's profile photo showed him on a motorcycle, geared up in leather, wearing a helmet and goggles. All Dave could make out was his nose, straight along the bridge, but swollen with cartilage. It looked powerful and a little sunburned. Just as Dave was about to scroll on to the next profile, Swingl hit him up: 'Hey Dave,' with an added tongue-sticking-out emoji.

Dave seized with anxiety. His first impulse was to block Swingl, but then what? He scanned the area in a 50 foot circumference, then 100 feet, then an even wider circle, but didn't see anyone who might be Swingl. He was scanning for that nose, for someone on his phone. It was the most alive he'd felt inside that coffin of a building.

'Hi. Who's this?' Dave replied, trying to sound cool.

'Howz MKE meet any QTs?'

Dave didn't know what to make of this. Was Swingl ignoring his question, or hadn't he seen it before asking his own? This person obviously wanted something of him, even if it was the vicarious pleasure of hearing about his hook-ups. Maybe Swingl just wanted to taunt him. Knowing so little about him was unsettling, but knowing there was someone like him among the bikers was electric. Dave replied:

'Been nice—want to hear about it? Have we met?'

'YES please.'

'Ok. What will you tell me about you?'

"Nah but yr name's on yr shirt.'

There was a pause as Swingl's replies caught up to Dave's questions.

'Hehe. I'll show U under my 1-piece...'

It was a provocative offer. Dave texted a recap of his first night in Milwaukee, omitting the detail of Other Dave's stature. It seemed too much to give away. How many gay dwarves could there be in Milwaukee? Swingl replied by sending another photo in the one-piece, but with the zipper down. It was cropped just above the mouth, showing Swingl's full lips, thick stubble, and just a peek of his hairy body beyond the zipper.

Then he told Swingl about Victor, who was probably still sleeping. Dave offered some details about their sexual encounter. Swingl replied with an approving 'mhhm', followed by the tongue emoji. Swingl next sent Dave a photo of him with the one-piece pushed down. Dave made out a shoulder, a pec, and an ear in profile. It was enough to get Dave to delve into intimate details about Victor: his furry ass, his broad feet, his panther-like skull. He omitted the part about the sadness. Swingl in return sent Dave a short video file of him dropping the one-piece to the ground with his back to the camera and pulsing his juice cans. Dave did not know you could send videos over the app, and nearly swooned right there in the Wisconsin Convention Center, although the low airflow likely contributed to his feeling of light-headedness.

With that, Swingl was gone. He'd either blocked Dave or deleted his account. Dave sought to regain his composure, but spent the afternoon scanning the lumbering crowds for that nose: so many large bodies, like a beast herd raised for butchering. Dave felt anxiety about how the silos of his existence could have crumbled. Yet it was liberating to imagine what life could be like if his colleagues were to know. Maybe he could keep his job.

Dave decided to lay off the app on his last night after this risky interaction. He took an aimless wander along the Riverwalk then drifted off into the unknown, past brewery complexes and over train tracks. He came upon a farmer's market. The vendors were closing up for the day, but at a cheesemonger's table under a striped canopy, the goods were still out. The table was manned by two strapping young activist/farmers with full beards. They were so earnest about their organically fed animals and their small-batch approach. Dave fell in love with the cheesemongers while lamenting that he'd found nothing in this life to be so earnest about when he was their age—or even now. Those young men made things every day. He bought a little wheel of sheep's milk cheese, which he was told was "buttery, with a salty finish." He had no idea when he'd have occasion to eat it.

The next afternoon, following that museum tour, Dave made his way to the airport, with his branded backpack on this back, wheeling his branded rolling luggage through long corridors, carrying his artisan cheese in a brown bag. He recalled the perky museum guide from that afternoon's tour with annoyance. After walking the group through the company's technological advancements by the decade, she blabbed about how leveraged and recognizable the brand was, how it was in hundreds of product categories: outdoor furniture, golf clubs, phone cases. Then she said something Dave found most irksome: "Yet it still represents a spirit of rebellion to our customers!"

This public relations pablum made Dave want to zip out of the one-piece of his own skin and announce to the pack of big bodies obediently following Miss Perky that he'd been hooking up all over town. He didn't care who knew anymore. He even hooked up with a dwarf!

A brown-skinned Genius! And two cheesemongers! (Okay, that didn't actually happen). In his internal fury, Dave interrupted her spiel, bursting out of complacent silence. To the guide: "I cross more lines than you can draw, Miss Perky." To the other tour-goers: "One of your sons showed me his ass." Back to Miss Perky: "How's that for technological advancement? How's that for rebellion?"

Dave was relishing his moment, imaginary though it was, as he trudged through the airport. The internal dialog muted the grinding of his luggage wheels against the terrazzo and the metronomic swing of the bag of cheese and took him out of time and place. All he could manage was to follow the arrows pointing towards his gate. It seemed like he was rolling through the same corridor on a loop, past the same black chairs, past the same digital screen, blinking the same departure data.

Then a sight in the distance knocked Dave back to consciousness: a Harley-clad posse boarding Delta flight 4445 to Detroit. Repeated on two young men talking to one another, and there once more, on an older man who surely must be their father, was that nose, large, straight, and ample. Just as they were handing their tickets to the gate agent, Dave yelled abruptly, something you really shouldn't do in airports these days:

"Swingl!"

One of the young men—in a style of sunglasses Dave had been selling—cocked his head in Dave's direction, grinning, and gave him a biker salute, its trajectory arcing along the space frame and landing right in Dave's throat, before disappearing into the jetway. Struck with a wave of self-consciousness for his outburst, Dave scanned the terminal for TSA agents. He sheepishly made his way to his gate and threw his luggage and himself on the carpet as jet fumes spiked his senses. He didn't even notice that his flight was listed as delayed. Every time he got someone next to him—in a wooden house, in a hotel room, under a space frame—it's like the satellites ruled and his longings got stranded deep in the exosphere. He opened the crumpled bag and the tang of the cheese released, conjuring a vision of grass pastures dotted with ovine clouds. Dave took a bite of the cheese, warm and runny, and waited for the promised finish.

BENNY ABOARD

How Benny found himself on a train—bound for nowhere and down-ing a handful of sleeping pills—was an instance of a bad day gone worse. On his last train trip, he was presenter for a pharmaceutical company, having boarded in Atlanta and disembarked in Birmingham. He'd made his way to the upscale steak restaurant he'd booked for his last gig, a dinner presentation was planned for a group of doctors, to enlighten them on the benefits of Luminda, a sedative used to treat mild insom-nia. Now he was out of a job and out of fucks.

Though the restaurant wasn't far from the main hospital, most of the invited had had to travel through downtown to get there. A protest rally had been planned along Fourth Avenue that evening. Traffic was blocked for several hours until the protesters were arrested. "What do they want now," Benny had joked nervously to the few attendees who'd made it through, mopping his brow of sweat. Looking at the mirrored wall, he straightened his tie and assessed his appearance: still passably attractive, although he winced at his receding hairline and the dark cir-cles under his bright eyes. The scar on his chin from the accident was not visible thanks to some concealer. He gave the presentation to barely one-third of his RSVP list. His boss was annoyed–their drug compa-ny client would challenge him over the increased cost per person–and hurled complaints at Benny over the phone. "A good rep plans for all contingencies, Benny...You've got to be a ninja of logistics," he railed.

A certain Doctor Shamda had interrupted Benny's rote presentation with challenges to the studies he'd cited. "There's a much greater incidence of suicidal ideation associated with long-term use of Luminda than your data lets on," she stood up and announced just as he was getting to the bar charts. "There's not nearly enough about alcohol interaction...you're whitewashing the problem," she'd carried on stridently, as Benny sought to calmly counter her arguments. She cited data points he didn't understand from peer-reviewed studies with which he was unfamiliar. Benny had never had a doctor go off on him like that. He had meticulously planned all aspects of the meeting—the venue, the menu, the slide show, the literature packets, the sample kits—but was not prepared to be challenged on its content. *Most of them just nod politely and eat their fucking steaks...*

He'd left the restaurant worried, a bag of steak dinners in takeout containers scant consolation. Hurrying to the station to catch the train, his wheeled suitcase bounced over cracked sidewalks. One of its wheels loosened along the way, causing it to rack and squeal. One on board the train, he settled into his music—but then his boss called again, railing about a video. "What video?" Apparently Doctor Shamda had livestreamed her rant to her surprisingly large following.

"They want you off the contract. You can head straight home. I gotta scramble for a sub in Tuscaloosa."

"But..the train..." Benny grasped at the words to explain.

"Sorry, Benny. Drug company decision. I'll get you on another tour soon," he said, hanging up before Benny could get it out.

Benny was undone. He'd been on the Luminda gig for the last month, having figured out the travel logistics without his car, and had finally gotten the full presentation committed to memory. He'd earn a week's less pay and lose the remaining travel per diem. The train was heading away from home. He then remembered he couldn't even go home if he wanted to. He'd rented his apartment to a couple from New York who were visiting Atlanta for a wedding. He'd stashed all of his personal items, left the place sparking clean, and even put together a welcome basket.

The ticket agent came by, and Benny asked, "Sir, what's the final destination for this train?"

"This here's the Crescent, son. New Orleans. Pulls in late tonight."

"Can I change my reservation to go all the way?" asked Benny, pushing forth his ticket.

"Check online," he replied. Benny looked around at the nearly empty car, then looked back at him. "You don't know who's boarding up ahead," he advised. Benny did as he said, and found he was able to change his destination for an additional charge—a bit more than he'd hoped. Flashing his new e-ticket, the agent nodded.

Benny saw no better option than spending the weekend in New Orleans. He'd have to watch his expenses seeing as he'd just lost his gig, but he had enough coming in from the last month to justify a little adventure. Outside of Tuscaloosa, he locked eyes with a truck driver stopped at the crossing, and resolved to stray outside of his comfort zone, to take chances, to act on impulse. He offered steak dinners to a family seated in the middle of the car and they were delighted. Then he dug through his sample kits and popped four Lumindas out of their blister packs. *Fuck your suicidal ideation*, he muttered as he threw them back with a nip of whiskey.

He slept fitfully. The ticket agent shook him awake just as the train pulled in to its final destination and gave him a stern look. There was a mess of food scattered around his seat, like a small animal had ransacked one of the steak dinners, along with several empty bottles. His tray table was pooled with soda. "Union Station, New Orleans," the agent hollered, and directly to Benny said gruffly, "Clean up after yourself, son." Benny gave him a confused look. He didn't remember eating anything last night and he had no idea where the soda had come from. He quickly cleaned up and hurried off the train.

He boarded a streetcar to the edge of the French Quarter then trooped through the Quarter along Dauphine Street. It was a rainy night and he ducked under canopies along the way, his wobbly suitcase squeaking louder with each block. He walked to the Marigny where he'd booked a room last minute. The guesthouse had some questionable reviews but advertised as gay-friendly.

The manager of the guesthouse stubbed out her cigarette and rolled the box up in her shirt sleeve upon seeing Benny approach. She projected the taut masculinity of James Dean. "I'm Kay, welcome to the Marigny," she said, assertively shaking Benny's hand and throwing his suitcase over her shoulder. As she walked him up to his room, she rattled off neighborhood options for eating and drinking. "There's a Vietnamese counter in the back of the Love Lounge, everyone gets brunch at Who Dat, and if you're looking for strong coffee, Orange Couch on the corner," she said, handing him the key. "Sounds inviting," answered Benny. Kay nodded and left him to his room, and Benny collapsed on the dented mattress.

The room was spare, the furnishings mismatched. It was the front room of the top floor and had once been a sitting room. There was a pair of parlor doors separating it from the back of the house, now fixed, their lights now covered over with plywood. The night in a strange room brought him disturbed sleep. He had the repeated sensation of falling through the sky, except he felt gravity pulling downward towards his feet. He dreamt of nodding off behind the wheel of a rental car, the one he'd driven in Jacksonville, a Chevy Volt. He'd wake up in a panic to find the car careening towards an embankment along a river. Although he was still asleep; the feeling of waking to find himself having lost control of the vehicle was the conclusion of the recurrent nightmare.

He was awakened for real shortly after dawn by the crowing of a rooster, which he found more disorienting than annoying. He pieced together the evidence he could gather with one opened eye upon his surroundings, the sink of the mattress beneath him, and his blurred recall of yesterday's events. "New Orleans," he intoned. He remembered a certain James Dean character mentioning coffee on the corner and something about a couch? He showered and dressed, making an effort to style his thinning hair after the James Dean character.

The Orange Couch was a coffee bar filled with shiny young laptop warriors, with the exception of one table of dapper older men with pronounced southern drawls. Benny admired their stylish attire as he took the open table next to theirs. He was settling into the establishment's familiar hipster vibe when one of the men began discussing politics.

"I saw a report last night that proves it. Obama *is* a radical Muslim..."

His friend's face registered dismay.

Benny exclaimed, "Hah!" He turned to the man and said, "I don't believe you're that gullible. You're in on it." The old man blinked at Benny as if he'd farted and resumed his conversation. Benny noisily got up from the table, and finding no other available seats, took his coffee outside. While fumbling for his sunglasses, he vented about the man's politics to a young woman with long braids seated at the outdoor table. As she lent him a sympathetic ear, a cock with magnificent plumage—a golden crest, deep blue tail feathers—strutted by. Benny stopped his venting to stare.

"Oh, that's Boney. He live around here," the young woman said.

The bird continued his strut up Royal street, attracting the attention of a pack of pastel-clad tourists venturing into the neighborhood in search of Who Dat. They burbled their delight and stalked Boney with their camera phones, while the locals treated him with the casual indulgence of a neighbor who repeats his stories.

Benny drank his coffee in silence and left the young woman to her reading. The intermittent rain cast off ozone he eagerly inhaled as he walked uptown with a plan to tour the homes of the Garden District. As he crossed under the Pontchetrain Expressway he scurried past an encampment of homeless veterans. Their makeshift enclosures of soggy shipping boxes were encircled with overfilled shopping carts, hung with bags ballooning with empty bottles and cans. One man pacing outside the encampment made menacing gestures at him.

A woman in a floral print dress conducted the tour; she habitually pursed her lips between descriptions. The menace in front of the homeless encampment intruded on his contemplation of the first home's curated interiors, and the tour guide's enthusiasm for its genteel domesticity struck him as laced with cruelty. He returned to the guesthouse with sore feet and threw himself face down on the bed. Sharp noises filled his room—from the sounds of it, a guest in a drunken rampage beyond the parlor doors, slurring and knocking things down. Benny put on his headphones and opened Grindr.

After rounds of elliptical chat he was approached by a young man from about twenty miles away. Darios was a Creole blend of African, Native, and French, according to his description. 'I'm a country boy who can't stay out of the city,' read his quote. Benny found his messages honest and funny: 'SO R U down for some fun? It's been a minute for me,' he wrote, with the winking emoji. He was a ramp agent at the airport and lived with his family in Luling. Benny fell asleep before he could answer.

In the morning, he again crossed paths with Boney, who strutted Royal Street with the nonchalant air of a prince surveying his domain. He followed the bird as he turned onto Mandeville Street. A local greeted the bird with repeated cries of "Where y'at, Boney?" As Benny tilted his head to figure out what the man was saying, Boney slipped through a gate. Benny scurried over to the gate and peered into the yard.

An older woman in a long white dress was sitting on a lawn chair. She said something incomprehensible to Benny, the last word of which was "bébé." She laughed, and pushed her hand through the air for emphasis. He thought for a moment she'd said his name and it startled him. Her face changed and she summoned him to come closer. Benny leaned on the gate and it swung open, so he walked towards her. "Koki, I am not pressed, if I have a coup..." she said into his neck, and then her eyes lowered towards a tree stump in the yard. Benny was confused. A cloth lay over the flat of the stump and the base was wrapped in beads. On the cloth was a bone, a candle, a rock, and a painted doll. Boney pecked at the doll. Benny understood that he was to give a tribute, so he pulled some bills out and set them under the rock. The woman laughed, and Boney skittered off.

He hadn't fully understood his interaction with the woman in the long white dress, but it left him feeling somewhat better about his circumstances. Walking back to the guesthouse, he opened Grindr again and invited Darios to visit. He wouldn't ordinarily hook up with a stranger, and he'd only ever been with one other man with brown skin. Vincent was the roommate he'd been assigned as a freshman at Emory, an athlete from Cascade Heights. They'd slept in the same bed one night when Vincent's bed got flooded by a broken pipe upstairs, and it led to some furtive stroking neither had ever acknowledged.

After they exchanged numbers, Darios texted to say he'd borrow his dad's car and drive into town. It took him hours to arrive, and Benny came close to falling asleep a few times. Darios finally appeared wearing pressed pants and a varsity sweater, apologizing for the delay. "First I couldn't figure out what to wear," he said, which struck Benny as funny, considering they'd probably be taking off their clothes anyway. Darios confessed to having had second thoughts a few miles out of Luling.

"I pulled over and turned back around. Then I thought better of it. Then I had to stop for gas in Metairie."

Darios was outgoing, rangy, and electric. He lit up when Benny mentioned the Garden District. "I took a guided tour one day. The homes I did see." They engaged in a far-reaching chat about work, family, sex, and New Orleans history. Darios hardly kept still through it, pacing the room, waving his hands as he spoke. Benny could easily picture him on the tarmac directing large aircraft to their gates, signaling with those orange batons. Darios tried to convey the care he'd taken in getting there: driving a good car at night, selecting a gas station, parking away from the bar on the next corner, dressing like a college student. "You know, round here you've got to do things just right," he said. Benny failed to understand, assuming he was just being provincial. Then Darios asked, "Are you waiting on me to make a move? Cuz I'm shy in that way."

Benny pulled in to him and kissed him softly. They wrested each others' clothes off and found each others' tender spots. Darios kissed Benny's neck and even gave him a little bite on the earlobe. No one had ever found his spot, just behind the ear, so quickly, and he was instantly turned on like a switch. His moaning grew louder with every touch from Dario's hot skin so Darios put his hand over his mouth. He worried that they might attract attention. In the darkened room, Benny's eyes returned over and again to the reddish glow of Darios' skin as the porch light filtered through the broken louvers.

As their lust mounted, Benny's noisiness was muted by Darios' caution. Benny inhaled deeply as Darios' hand edged up under his nostrils. It was smoky with a hint of leather, possibly from his dad's car. After their prolonged round of sexual acrobatics, during which Benny tacked between euphoria and exhaustion, Benny collapsed over Darios on the mattress, now teetering in one corner, having been knocked off its frame.

"You can stay over if you like," said Benny. After the long wait and their exhausting session, he was crashing hard and would take the path of least resistance. "I've got to get the car back to my dad," Darios explained as he dressed in his college student attire. Benny roused himself enough to stand and hugged his visitor goodbye.

Darios came upon a startled Kay on the front porch and gave her a cautious nod. Kay dragged on her cigarette and narrowed her eyes at him. "Evening," she said. Darios mumbled a reply. Kay stubbed out her cigarette and went back inside, checking the lock on the front door. Darios noted the rowdy crowd spilling out of the corner bar and crossed the street to get to his car.

Benny slept on the tilted mattress like he hadn't in weeks, physically spent, his sore head flooded with happiness charges. He kept his hand under his nose so he could smell Darios' skin and their sex.

For his last day in New Orleans Benny took a bike ride. Kay had offered him one of the guesthouse's loaners. "Great way to see the Lower Ninth," she'd said. "Biking's easy here, you know, being flat." He rolled through the surrounding neighborhoods, encountering very few people in the streets all day. Someone seemed to be closing a door or disappearing around a corner everywhere he cycled. He returned the bike to Kay that evening and thanked her.

"It's my pleasure," Kay said, lighting another cigarette.

"You were so right, such a great way to get around," his enthused. The cycling had done his body good.

"That's it." She inhaled and blew a couple of smoke rings. "Now, about last night..."

Benny's pleasant feelings evaporated.

"You just want to take care about who you have over here. You never know..."

"He's a college student," Benny protested, though falsely. The James Dean mask dropped from Kay's face and she scrunched her face with defensive petulance.

"I'm just looking out for you. We've had incidents here..."

"Of course. Thank you." Benny said, and went to his room.

It was a hot night and his last exchange with Kay left him seething in resentment. *How could she?* he muttered as he swept a pile of his belongings off the nightstand and into his suitcase. The last of the sample kit blister packs crackled in his hand.

Benny's narcotic sleep was punctuated with dreams about the stranded vistas he'd taken in on the bike ride: the blank seawall at the end of Spain Street, the long flatness looking down towards the levee known as The End of the World. A familiar pattern to his dreams emerged. He'd be floating through these areas as if on air, with no people around, and then he would be sucked out of the scene as if down a drain and he'd be back before the woman in the long white dress. She'd tell him something he couldn't understand, something he sensed he needed to know. Halfway through the night, she said something he understood, and it startled him awake.

Benny gathered up his nips of liquor and made his way to the front porch. It was the only time he'd found the porch without Kay. Menace seemed to pour off the men hanging outside the corner bar so he walked in the other direction. He downed a whiskey and took Mandeville again—like on the day he'd first encountered the woman in the white dress—and wandered until he came upon a school. The gate to the schoolyard was open and he entered, squinting to make out the graffiti on a concrete barrier in the incidental light. Stumbling along the yard's perimeter, he downed a vodka. His forward foot kicked at something soft with a thud. As he bent down to examine it, the stench of rot overwhelmed his nostrils. It was Boney, or seemed to be in the dark. He backed away from the corpse with a start.

"Who did this?" he cried through tears. The sight of the magnificent rooster lying wet and limp in the gravel brought out all his misery. He used the light in his phone to illuminate the scene. The little corpse was teeming with maggots. "But how?" he demanded. He remembered enough from his year of pre-med to know that maggots took at least three days to appear on a corpse. *This can't be Boney,* he reasoned. *Or could the heat and humidity have accelerated the timeline of decay?* He set his empty nip bottles around the corpse as a kind of improvised altar and stumbled back to the guesthouse.

He was awaken by the sound of a dog scratching at the door. He'd seen a dog around the property but couldn't grasp whether it belonged to Kay, or was the house dog, or just a local stray. He cracked open the door but found the corridor empty. He dressed, dropped his room key in the check-out box, and made his way to the Orange Couch. Finding no older dapper gentlemen parroting conspiracy theories he sat inside. The sun was already strong and his head was pounding. He kept an eye out for Boney but the bird did not appear.

172

Benny downed a coffee and summoned a car to take him to the airport. He was rolling down the windows as they drove past the guesthouse. Kay, back on the porch, was berating a man who was having trouble standing up and holding steady. *That must have been the drunk I heard through the wall,* thought Benny. He checked in to his flight back to Atlanta. *There goes my vacation,* he'd griped when he'd booked the seat with the last of his frequent flyer points. His tenants were leaving that morning and they'd reported a pleasant stay. This one thing going right gave Benny solace.

The driver laughed at the sight of Kay ejecting the drunken man. His old Pontiac, lacking proper suspension, swayed and bounced along on the route to Louis Armstrong International. Despite the less-than-smooth ride, Benny passed out in the back seat. He didn't notice when his phone rang and the call went to voicemail.

At the same time Darios was driving his father's car to the airport to get to his shift. He'd borrowed the car that day because he planned on meeting up with some friends on Magazine Street after work. He was pulled over by a Jefferson Parish policeman on suspicion of driving a stolen vehicle. He'd cooperated and showed him the registration in his father's name. When the policeman claimed there was an irregularity, Darios took out his phone to call his father. The policeman swatted the phone out of his hand, ordered him out of the car, and threw him against it to handcuff him. Darios' thumb dialed Benny's number just before the phone landed on the new floor mat he had bought for his dad.

His face hit the roof of his dad's Cadillac so hard his lip split. He pleaded his innocence, "Officer, this my father's car, call him," and licked his swelling lip. The policeman grabbed him by the nape and forced him into the back seat of his cruiser.

Roused by the driver at the airport, Benny made his way through security, boarded the plane, stashed his bag in the overhead compartment, and found the last of his nips. Noticing the voicemail alert, he listened to the accidental recording. He could barely make out Darios' pleas, the policeman's smug tone, and the sound of dirt kicking up. He played it again, then sucked in the recirculated air, horrified. As he hit the call back button, the flight attendant set his seat back in the upright position and instructed him to put his phone in airplane mode. Benny pantomimed compliance while the phone rang but it did not connect.

DONOR BABY

On the appointed morning, Teddy trimmed his graying beard, put on a button-down shirt which had grown a bit tight since he'd last worn it, and trudged down to the criminal court building, an imposing Art Deco heap with four towers surrounding a central ziggurat. Though what was before him filled most New Yorkers with dread, he welcomed the break in his routines and was even a little turned on by civic spaces. What he hadn't anticipated was the assault on his composure of the morning rush hour subway trip. Chewed up by the legion of elbowing commuter warriors and spit out at City Hall Station, he gathered himself once inside the paneled courtroom, holding his tall frame upright and pulling in his belly.

He sat with a pool of potential jurors opposite the defendant, a handsome young man with red-brown skin and an indifferent air accused of marijuana possession. *No one should be in jail over a plant,* Teddy fumed. Despite the young man's baggy clothes, Teddy caught peeks of his sinewy build as he shifted in his chair; he indulged a fleeting fantasy of smoking up and making out with him after convincing the rest of the jury to acquit.

The judge addressed the juror pool: "You must be completely honest in your answers to the attorneys. Don't hold back any detail, even if it seems irrelevant." Teddy was a little shaken. He was still resolved to lie but they didn't bring up his own marijuana use as he'd expected. Instead, he was asked coded questions about civil order and law enforcement. He gave the answers he thought would get him selected. Several potential jurors were dismissed. *I'm a semi-finalist*, he congratulated himself, breathing out, adjusting his imaginary sash.

In the next round of questioning, one of the lawyers asked, "Do you have any children?" He wondered about the relevance—maybe parents would be more authoritarian with suspected drug sellers? Or perhaps they'd have empathy for the young defendant? Remembering the judge's admonition, Teddy blurted out, "None that I know of..." There was laughter all around the room; even the defendant hooted. He hadn't meant it as snark; he was just being completely honest.

He was dismissed with the next batch of rejects.

The lawyer's question had prompted a panicked recall of his stint as a sperm donor. It was an episode he'd pushed out of his conscious mind for years. He was a broke college student and he'd get fifty dollars a pop at this lab uptown. He couldn't be sure in the spontaneous rush, but he thought maybe they'd made some babies from his donations. Up until that courtroom inquiry he'd put the whole enterprise out of his head; now, a surge of impressions hit as he loped away from the judicial ziggurat.

Navigating Canal Street, Teddy formed a mental picture of the ad he'd seen: business card size, with large copy reading SPERM DO-NORS and in smaller letters, a phone number. It was definitely in print; the Internet didn't even exist back then. He was pretty sure it was in the Village Voice: *That's where you'd find stuff like that.* The ad had enticed him with promises of quick and easy money. *Beats working, right?*

Teddy had called the number and answered a series of questions. He was then invited to the lab on Madison Avenue in the Fifties, a location which in Teddy's mind had lent the enterprise some legitimacy. He'd entered the building's lobby on the appointed day; polished marble gleamed and brass accents sparkled. The doorman seemed to know where he was headed and indifferently gestured towards a sign that read "ISOLD LABORATORIES," and pointed down a staircase.

The basement, with its bright white walls and greenish fluorescent lighting, was hygienic and pulsed with the audible buzz of mechanical systems. A young nurse had handled Teddy's intake, pretty and solid, but fairly stern and humorless. Strictly business, she was not remotely amused by the particulars of her assignment, and wore the skeptical scowl of a gatekeeper, looking out for any undesirables who might disturb this holy sanctum of reproductive science.

Teddy had been asked a series of questions by Nurse Stern, as he came to think of her. She'd marked down his responses on a form. The questions probed his background, general health, interests, and medical history. Then she looked up from her form and narrowed her eyes.

"Any homosexual inclinations?"

"No."

"Any activity?"

"None."

He'd intuitively known that any positive responses to these questions would have been a deal-breaker. Though he'd dated girls through his junior year, in high school he'd been seduced by a male classmate late one summer night, after taking a midnight dip in someone's pool. Mickey was flamboyantly gay, and had propositioned him as they huddled in bath towels. Teddy's wet Speedo bunched down around his ankles and his butt slipped between the plastic straps of the chaise lounge as Mickey gave him his first blow job. His gay encounters in college had been drunken and furtive, but he was pretty sure by then where they were leading.

It had come time to collect Teddy's first donation. Nurse Stern, who sat on the other side of a Lucite wall—just like in a money bank—slid a stack of porn magazines and a little cup through the deal tray. There was an issue of *Juggs*, a *Leg Show*, and one pretty hardcore title on the bottom. Teddy wordlessly pushed the porn back at her, keeping the cup. They glared at each other for a hot minute through the speak hole, then she pointed towards a small room with a bench and a counter.

He'd locked the door, opened his pants, closed his eyes, and willed his imagination to do better than those crumpled magazines. He came up with a pansexual frieze, bodies rolling onto one another, a procession of sexually peaking individuals hungry for his touch. It took no time at all and the main challenge was aiming for the cup.

His sample had been rigorously tested. "You've got a very high sperm count…your sample demonstrates excellent motility," the lab assistant enthused.

"Tell me something I don't know," Teddy crowed. "Wait, what is that?"

"Motility measures how active your little swimmers are. You need a high score for fertility treatments."

"Okay, cool…" He recalled signing off on some paperwork, only briefly glancing at the terms.

"Your samples may be used either for fertilization or research. They'll be frozen; that's why motility is important…"

"Frozen?"

Initially lured by the promise of easy money, Teddy had suddenly become concerned about the science. There'd be no way for him to be sure how his donations were used. His worry was fleeting; cash ruled. Once he was officially registered as a donor, he scheduled an appointment right away. He was eager to get the income flowing. Nurse Stern informed him that he could only donate twice a month. He'd envisioned it becoming his primary income; instead it became a supplement to a part-time job at a copy shop. He'd go to the clinic every other week for about eight months until he couldn't face the disapproving scowl of Nurse Stern once more. She was always there, someone he simply couldn't charm, and she seemed to suspect him.

This buried episode surged back into his consciousness as Teddy made his way home through clotted streets. He wrinkled his nose at a loud man ahead of him bad at sharing the sidewalk. *Ugh, this obnoxious suit, can't wait to get home.* Locking the door, he shucked his grown-up clothes, sprawled naked on the sofa, and processed: *Maybe I really do have children, they'd be grown by now, a whole army...* The cat settled on the sofa's arm, purring loudly.

◆

"Going on a run," Minnie yelled up to her mom, throwing shades on over her warm brown eyes. As she passed the neighbor's blooming jasmine hedge, tentacles of its fragrance grasped at her inhalations. Minnie wasn't an enthusiastic runner, but on this visit, it was the best way out of the house. Like the jasmine, her mother was in full flower and best in small doses. *The fawning is a little intense this trip,* she thought as a power-walker serpentined towards her.

Lola, who'd raised mostly Minnie mostly on her own, still had that ease in her body and feline good looks that drew men's attention. She strained not to pop the top button of her fitted vest while watching the art handler bring in some old photos she'd had professionally printed and framed. Pablo, a shaggy-haired artist from Silver Lake, wore white gloves; he was charged with hanging the photos in the living room in a pleasing composition.

"You're very tall…that must come in handy in your field," said Lola.

"Doesn't hurt," answered Pablo as he unwrapped the largest photo. The photos were printed in Kodachrome colors, their frames finished to resemble driftwood.

Lola stifled a *You're looking thin, honey* upon Minnie's return, pushing breakfast rolls on her instead. Minnie's face registered surprise at the presence of the art handler but she was glad to have a buffer. In the first picture he hung, Lola stood proudly in front of the house, bearing down on a shovel. A man was visible through the front window; he'd always been a shadow to Minnie, like several others. This particular shadow had given Lola the then-dilapidated house.

"How was your run? I don't remember you being such a runner…"

"Great! Went all the way through Nichols Canyon."

Pablo mapped out his composition with some blue tape on the stucco wall, planning a casual-seeming array. The next photo to go up was a shot of Lola and two of her friends, taken in the backyard of the place in Venice Beach. Minnie smiled at the sight of these women; they used to watch her during Lola's shifts after she'd left Minnie's dad. Lola and her friends worked at Cheetahs in Hollywood, one club where they could make good money and run their own schedules, at least until the game changed.

"Do you remember Kitty? That's her leaning on the handrail. She used to make our costumes," asked Lola.

"Sure I remember Kitty. She made my purple sequined headband with the feather."

"Of course. You wore that all through first grade!"

"Kitty was a hugger." The other woman in the photo was Aunt Robin.

"Do you remember taking naps on the porch with little Jamal? Aunt Robin would sing "State of Independence." It was one of her go-to numbers, *that* you wouldn't have known. She sang it to you two like a lullaby, lower and lower until sleep came on."

The next picture Pablo selected showed Lola's dad holding baby Minnie.

"Your dad was the club bag man. I fell for him against my better judgement..."

"Yeah, you've told me..."

"He was *so* sweet with me. You'd never know it to look at him. He wanted me to quit the business and settle down."

"And you took him up on it."

"I wasn't strictly against it, but I wanted it on my terms, not for a man on a savior trip."

"Right on mom," Minnie replied with a raised fist.

"One day he came over with a rock in a box and went down on one knee..."

"It's the only photo of dad I've ever seen him smiling," said Minnie.

"I tell you, sweetie, that big lug floated on air when you were born..."

"Last one in this group," Pablo said as he hung a fourth photo, of Lola with her mother holding an infant Minnie. He'd arranged the photos in chronological order, but rather than in a line, it was more of a radiating spiral.

"Grandma Lovie," said Minnie. Lola went silent.

In the photo, Grandma Lovie stands leaning away from Lola, disapproval scaffolding her face. It looks like she's holding the infant *away* from her body. Minnie noticed her mother's eyes welling with tears, threatening to undo her eyeliner.

Lola shuffled over to her pot stash and packed a bong. She drew in, then held her wedding ring in the light.

"Do you like what Pablo is doing with the photos?" asked Lola through an exhale.

"They look great, mom."

"This is me getting right with my past, Minnie. Nothing to hide anymore. Dancing–stripping–gave me so much. It gave me you. It gave me the means to raise you. Sammy, bless his broken soul. This house, which I rebuilt from a wreck." Drawing a second hit, words rushed her throat on the exhale. "Sweetie…I need to tell you something. Much as Sammy is your dad, he's not in one sense…"

"What?"

"In the biological. He couldn't have kids, so we went to a fertility clinic in Santa Monica and…"

"You what?" The surprise got the better of Minnie.

Lola continued: "He's your father because he took the initiative. He raised you until we split, and he pays for your college, the whole bill."

"You never told me…"

"How could we explain? And it didn't seem fair once we broke up. It was his idea. The clinic got donors from New York because they had stricter standards. We picked a donor that matched him in height, hair color, and such. He held my hand…"

"So who's my dad? I want to know…" Minnie was already working out the travel logistics, the airport shuttle, the flight, to set eyes on him.

"Honey… they don't disclose donors' names…"

Minnie sipped her coffee quietly and tore off pieces of pastry instead of fighting with her mother. Years of little lies swarmed her thoughts like cicadas, though it was a relief to know at least part of the truth. Some incongruent details, like Sammy's blood type, like the things Lola called him when they had that screaming fight, made sense now. This whole puzzle-piece realignment of the past, however, was background noise to the overwhelming urge to meet her biological father.

Her mind raced with questions as she showered and dressed. On her way down for a day of shopping and soft recriminations with her mother, Pablo cornered her.

"You're Minnie, right? I'm Pablo."

"Hey Pablo, awesome job on the photos."

"Thanks! This one's going up over the couch, wait 'til you see."

He picked up the largest of the photos, showing Lola and Robin hanging on one another in the back of Cheetahs. They were wearing stilettos, sequined panties and plain white t-shirts. A toddler–Minnie–was hanging on Robin's leg.

"So hey, and so sorry for eavesdropping, but you should know…"

"About my father?"

With his long fingers in the air, Pablo indicated the spot on the wall reserved for the larger photo, and continued:

"Yeah, there's a new law for donor babies and it applies to you."

"So that's what I am? A *donor baby*…"

Pablo hung the large photo over the couch, opposite the grouping. It was landscape format shot low with the ladies standing in the middle of the parking lot, the club's red-orange wall and its metal fire stair behind them.

"Yeah, adult donor children can request information about the father. I keep up on the subject; my sister asked me to be a donor for her and her girlfriend."

"You have a son?" asked Minnie.

"Well, I'm a gay uncle," Pablo showed Minnie a photo of the boy on his phone. "Conner is six. Sometimes he calls me 'Uncle Daddy.'"

"Wow, he's adorable…So what should *I* do?" she asked.

Before handing her the key that could unlock her past, Pablo returned his focus to the large photo. "Meiselas— she's a total badass."

Minnie inspected the photo. "I've never seen this one. It's like the two of them are starting a world of their own…hey, that's me," Minnie's eyes welled over as Pablo gushed admiration.

Later that afternoon, Minnie drove Lola back from their shopping day. Packages filled the back seat, while in the front they avoided difficult subjects.

Lola folded down the visor and applied lipstick in the mirror.

"Mom, I'm glad you're putting out the photos. You know I'm proud of you…" Minnie hadn't always been so accepting of her choices.

She turned to her daughter, clearly moved. "I can't do secrets any more, Minnie. They're *killing* me."

"Okay mom, calm down…" They broke into laughter, then pulled up to the driveway Lola had repaved over a hot weekend.

"There's a new law, I can request the donor's identity," said Minnie. "But you need to tell me where to start…"

Lola stepped out of the car and fussed with a potted plant on the front porch as Minnie retrieved the packages from the back seat.

"Are you sure?"

"You'd want to know…"

Lola opened the door. "I kept a form from the lab, if they're even still in business. I'll dig it up."

"Thanks, mom!" Minnie smiled brightly and kissed her. "No more secrets, right?"

Minnie changed her return flight for a small charge. Upon landing at LaGuardia, she navigated her carry-on past construction areas, then took the subway straight to ISOLD Laboratories, carrying the form Lola had given her like a divining rod. She met with an administrator—the very same woman who Teddy used to called Nurse Stern. Her real name was Donna and she was as guarded with Minnie as she had been with Teddy.

"Your donor has not signed a release form and without that, I can't disclose his identity," Donna said as she closed the file.

"Have you given him the form?"

"They weren't in use then," replied Donna dismissively.

"So you can send him one," Minnie pleaded with her eyes.

"I only have the address he gave us back then…It's unlikely…"

"Try. Nothing to lose," replied Minnie, smiling irresistibly.

◆

A month later, as she was strolling across campus, Minnie received a call from Donna: "Your donor's form came back." As Minnie wrote down 'Theodore Brick' and the address of her biological father, she resisted the urge to discern character from his name. Minnie thanked Donna profusely, melting her cold, protective veneer. She bought a train ticket to New York for the following Friday.

The address was a tenement building in Hell's Kitchen with an old-school Italian grocer on the ground floor. The building, though clean and well maintained, was a holdout alongside high-rises flying flags promoting luxury rentals and various amenities: roof decks, gyms, concierge services. She could hardly make out names or numbers on the rusty intercom, so she took her best guess, hit a button, and got buzzed in. As she scaled the narrow staircase to the top, she realized with foreboding: *My father lives in a fifth-floor walk-up...*

On the fourth floor, an elderly lady peered at her from behind a latched door, muttering curses in Spanish. Cooking smells and salsa music on the radio snuck past her. Minnie made it to the top landing, huffing a bit, and knocked on the door marked 5R. Like his neighbor, Teddy was cooking and playing music; "Don't You Want Me" by Human League blasted through his railroad flat and he was lip-syncing to Susan Ann Sulley's vocals in a high camp manner when he heard the second, louder knock.

"Hello?" Teddy said as he looked over Minnie.

"Hi, I'm Minnie. The lab gave me your name, umm..." She took in the fit bear of a man who'd answered the door in gym shorts and an apron that read 'Hot Stuff Coming Through.'

"Oh. OH! Come on in, wait let me..." Teddy lunged to lower the music, tripping over a garden hose which ran from the kitchen sink out the window, and then turned back to the kitchen to pull a baking tray out of the oven. Minnie let herself in and took a seat at the small kitchen table.

Teddy took the other chair, and the two of them looked at each other for a long time in silence, scanning each others' features. Teddy murmured with recognition at the brow line, the gold flecks around her pupils. *She has my eyes, my mouth...that must be her mother's nose, thankfully*, thought Teddy. He reached to touch her head, tentatively, until Minnie leaned into his caress.

"So you've been living here for a while, huh?" asked Minnie, breaking the spell.

"Oh yea, well, rent stabilized, I'll never leave," replied Teddy.

"I like what you've done with the place," she said, looking over the apartment. Over the years, Teddy had demolished the partitions and installed a big window unit facing the block's rear yards. The windows were open and a light breeze came through. His art work hung on the stripped-down walls.

"Thanks! Cupcake?"

"Thanks," replied Minnie, taking one.

"Oh, here," said Teddy as he applied frosting. He frosted the rest of the batch as Minnie ate hers.

"So...thanks for meeting me."

"Of course," replied Teddy.

"So what made you become a donor?"

"Well, to be honest, I was a broke college kid. My parents paid tuition but I was on my own for the rest," he replied.

"Oh," reacted Minnie, glumly.

"I know, not such a great origin story, right?"

"Teddy, can I ask you...not to be rude, but, you're gay, right?"

"Oh, yeah!"

"So what were you doing..."

"Donating sperm? Well why not? It's not contagious."

"I didn't mean..."

"It's okay. I was dating girls back then, but I had already done some stuff with guys, too. Anyway they ran all kinds of tests."

"I mean... I want to know..." Minnie stammered.

"A year or so after, I met my first real boyfriend, Jake. We lived together here," he said.

"Oh, so..."

"He turned me out. I've been a practicing homosexual ever since, and I've really gotten the hang of it," he said, smiling.

"Are you still together?" She asked.

187

"Jake died in ninety-six," he replied.

"I'm so sorry."

"Yeah, we lost a lot of good ones."

He brought her some coffee. She was processing everything she'd heard and wrinkled her nose, an expression he often made himself. He marveled at this hint of genetic transmission.

"Hey, do you want to smoke some kind?"

"Hmm, I don't usually partake..." she replied. "My mom smokes, too." she added awkwardly. Teddy fumbled with his stash and a dish full of seeds he was collecting, putting them aside.

"You know, they wanted to screen me out—but I didn't think being gay made me any less a man, so I lied," he said.

"Do you mind if I look at your art work?"

"Go right ahead."

Minnie made her way to the back of the space, puzzling over the kitsch collages on the wall. Someone knocked on the door, and a panicked expression crossed Teddy's face as he lunged to answer it.

"Hey daddy," said a young man in a tank top as he wrapped himself around Teddy.

Teddy begged him off, saying: "I totally forgot to text you! Aaron, this is Minnie."

"Oh, company—I'll come back," replied Aaron. "Nice to meet you," he said, waving to Minnie. "Text me later," he said to Teddy, winking as he made a hasty exit.

"Did he call you *daddy?*" She asked.

"Yea, but not in that way..." he replied, seeking to lead Minnie to understanding. Her eyes flashed in realization.

"Wow, ok...I don't know if this was a good idea..."

"What? Do I disappoint you?"

"No, it's not that…" she said. "It's just…living in this walk-up forever, getting high, hooking up with young randos, making your introspective art…" she paced, kicking the garden hose. "What's with the hose? Wait, I'm not sure I want to know…"

"I was watering. I have a whole urban farm on the roof. Don't be gross," he replied.

"Me?" She asked, astonished.

"Look missy—this is my life. So sorry I'm not up to your standards. Yea, you have a gay dad. That ought to make you extra compassionate," he said, as he sat back down and scarfed another cupcake.

"It's not that you're gay, ugh. It's just…You're like an overgrown man-baby." She went towards window for some air and stumbling over the garden hose lost her footing. She tried to right herself, but this only made her stumble more, and she hit her head on the window frame.

Teddy ran over to her. "Are you all right?" Minnie shook her head yes. He rushed to get her a cold pack out of the freezer. He held it to the bump on her forehead as they made their way back to the table.

"I should go," said Minnie.

"That was a close one," he said with a sigh of relief, trying not to hear her.

"I'm sorry, I didn't mean to yell, I just…"

"It's okay, it's an emotional day."

"I'll be in touch," she said, handing him the ice pack. Teddy airdropped his contact info to her phone. He went in for an embrace but she half turned, giving him an ambivalent side-hug. Closing the door behind her, he sighed and beelined to his pot stash.

Teddy was buzzed on amazement in the days after meeting Minnie, only harshed by the regret that he hadn't handled it better: *I should've suggested we go out to a cafe, the park...* A couple of weeks later, he was elated to receive a text from her: *Hi Teddy, I'll be back in NYC to see this show, one of my mom's friends is in it. Would you like to meet me there? We could hang out after, too. Minnie.* He followed the link she'd sent and bought a ticket.

Robin, Lola's old friend from Cheetahs, was appearing in the Raw Sugar Revue, a burlesque showcase for women of color. Teddy found a seat just behind Minnie, enjoying the first set—a curvaceous feather fan dancer, a sultry strip-teaser who bumped her way out of a hooped gown, a robe, gloves, a fringed underskirt, a corset, and a bra, down to a thong and tasseled pasties, a gender-bending illusionist who took the stage as swaggering stud and revealed to a lingerie-clad vamp. Between sets, Robin, the emcee, said, "These fine ladies are reclaiming burlesque and taking back our power," to applause. In the second set, she took the stage with two women dressed as nineteenth century dancing girls and a male performer with a waxed mustache, costumed as a strongman in a wrestling leotard. Minnie briefly turned to Teddy and cocked an eyebrow. *That's sweet, she's thinking about me, that I'd enjoy the beefcake,* thought Teddy.

During the finale—an Afro-futuristic piece in which the dancing girls were revealed to be sexy robots—strobe lights went off. Teddy shielded his eyes, aware of his photosensitivity. As applause broke out in the audience, he returned his attention to the stage. He noticed Minnie was shaking; then her body stiffened. She let out a cry and slumped over just as everyone else around her was rising to applaud. Teddy jumped over the seat, picked her up, and bull-rushed her out of the theatre. He laid her down on a bench in a dark area of the lobby, and putting her on her side, rolled up his jacket to support her head, loosening the clothing around her neck. He made sure her breathing wasn't obstructed. After a few tense moments, Minnie opened her eyes and squinted at him.

"What happened? Ooh, my head…"

"You had a seizure. Because of the lights. Reflex epilepsy. It's never happened before?"

"No. How did you know?"

"I've gotten them too—it's genetic. How are you feeling?"

"My head hurts, but I think okay. Is it going to happen again?"

"Just avoid strobes and light shows, you should be fine."

Minnie stood up, slowly, and pulled herself together, checking herself in the mirror hanging above the bench. As the crowd streamed into the lobby, she led Teddy backstage to see Robin.

"Aunt Robin!" She cried.

"Baby girl! Look how grown you are," Robin gushed as she hugged Minnie tightly. Robin was in a loose robe, and her performance wig was off to one side, revealing her natural hair.

"The show—fabulous," said Minnie.

"Yes, I loved your number, the part with the splits and the booty pops, and the transformation…" Teddy enthused.

"Who's this?" Robin said to Minnie.

"Oh, Robin, this is Teddy, he's, ahh, well, as you know, I'm a 'donor baby'…"

"Oh! This is your…"

"Teddy," he said, finishing Robin's thought.

"A pleasure. I see the resemblance," she said, studying his features.

"She's prettier," joked Teddy.

"Should we get drinks?" asked Minnie.

"I can't drink and keep up with these young girls, darling," answered Robin. "I wish we were back home, I'd smoke some kind…"

"Oh, I got you," said Teddy.

"Well, hook Auntie Robin up!"

Teddy smiled, pulling out a joint, and said, "Welcome to New York." He lit it for Robin and after a nice hit, she asked, "So, Teddy, ever think your donor baby would show up on your doorstep?"

"I hadn't thought about it for years until recently, believe it or not, during jury duty. Then I got that form in the mail," said Teddy, as he exhaled. "Once in a while I'd tell somebody about it and they'd think I was joking." The male performer from the finale came over to give Robin a hug, and made eyes at Minnie while Teddy gawked. Teddy offered Minnie a hit.

"Should I? After what happened," she asked.

"Oh, hon, it's half the reason I'm a stoner—trust, it cuts down on the seizures." Minnie toked awkwardly and reacted dramatically to the effects.

"Seizures? What seizures?" asked Robin.

"She's okay, she has photosensitivity, like me, and the strobe light in the finale set it off," he explained.

"Oh baby girl! I had no idea. I am *so* sorry. Are you all right?" asked Robin, fawning over her.

"Yeah, I'm fine now. Teddy took care of me."

"It was nothing. I got good at caretaking with Jake..." he said.

"See, look at him! That's a good man," said Robin.

"He is," replied Minnie. She turned to Teddy: "I was wrong about you."

"It's okay, sweetie. But you were right, I am a—what did you call me?"

"Ugh. An overgrown man-baby?" she answered sheepishly.

"It's not shade, just the truth. I'm underemployed, I smoke way too much pot, I fuck around too much…I'm a gay cliché."

"Oop," said Robin.

"I mean…" said Minnie.

"But I helped make a beautiful baby, didn't I?" he asked with a big smile.

"That you did," said Robin.

"Thanks Teddy," said Minnie. "And thank you for making me."

"You make me too, Minnie," he said, and took her hand.

"Oh daddy," she said, laughing as they embraced.

"Sometimes we get the best results from flawed choices," Teddy said over Minnie's shoulder to Robin, who toked and nodded in agreement.

Printed in the USA
CPSIA information can be obtained
at www.ICGtesting.com
LVHW091808050124
767856LV00004B/128